AUTISM, THE INVISIBLE CORD

A SIBLING'S DIARY

BY BARBARA CAIN, MSW

MAGINATION PRESS WASHINGTON, DC

AMERICAN PSYCHOLOGICAL ASSOCIATION

Published by
MAGINATION PRESS
An Educational Publishing Foundation Book
American Psychological Association
750 First Street, NE
Washington, DC 20002

For more information about our books, including a complete catalog,
please write to us, call 1-800-374-2721, or visit our website at
www.apa.org/pubs/magination.

Cover design by Oliver Munday
Typeset by Circle Graphics, Columbia, MD
Printed by Worzalla, Stevens Point, WI

Library of Congress Cataloging-in-Publication Data

Cain, Barbara S.
Autism, the invisible cord : a sibling's diary / by Barbara Cain.
p. cm.

"An Educational Publishing Foundation Book."

Audience: 13-18.
ISBN 978-1-4338-1191-3 (hardcover : alk. paper) — ISBN 978-1-4338-1192-0
(pbk. : alk. paper) 1. Autistic children—Family relationships—Juvenile
literature. 2. Autism in children—Juvenile literature. I. American
Psychological Association. II. Title.
RJ506.A9C345 2013
618.92'85882—dc23

2012016053

Manufactured in the United States of America

First printing — June 2012
10 9 8 7 6 5 4 3 2 1

CONTENTS

OCTOBER: WINGNUTS AND WIDGETS

If you were to see him riding his bike, smiling in the wind, you'd never know. Ezra looks like any other sixth grader with faded jeans, turned-around cap, and a messy bunch of butterscotch-colored curls. You see, my brother *is* like any other eleven-year-old . . . except when he isn't. Like today.

We're standing on the corner waiting for the school bus already five minutes late. Most of us are hanging, flirting—Tyler, the new guy across the street is soooo cute—or reliving last week's football game. Not Ezra. My brother doesn't know how to wait. Ez is categorically against anything but NOW. On his Ezra clock, a five-minute delay is panic time, but ten minutes means NEVER. The bus will never come. He'll never get to school. The sky will never stop falling.

I'm talking with Zoe but keep one eye on my brother the whole time. Ezra is flapping his hands and circling, circling the oak tree. I tell him, "It's OK, Ez, the bus is on its way, it will be here soon, I promise." I'm not getting through. I swallow hard. Ezra keeps circling. I speak slowly and softly each time he rounds the tree. It makes no difference. He's ready to throw himself on the ground.

I glance at Tyler who's fixed on this lovely spectacle. Not exactly the kind of attention I was looking for! Then I get the "widgets," that nasty flip-flop feeling that hammers my stomach whenever I'm scared or teary or want to hide. Most of the time I can talk Ez down when he freaks out like this, but when fourteen sets of eyes are staring and one pair belongs to Tyler . . . I freeze. Now Ezra is having an honest-to-goodness, state-of-the-art meltdown. He hurls himself against the tree and hollers like a screech owl. And I mean howls you could hear in Morocco.

From the corner of my eye, I see that nasty, scruffy-looking kid who is mean to everyone and everything. Zoe calls him the wingnut. He's inching closer. Ez is oblivious. My widgets are not. The kid plows into Ezra who in turn knocks into me. Now we're both lying on the ground in a heap when the bus arrives. Ez, always worried he'll be left behind, jumps to his feet, and is of course the first to climb aboard. We get in the bus and flop on the same seat. I'm totally exhausted and the day has only just begun.

Welcome to the neighborhood, Tiger, or Tyler, or whatever-your-name-is.

That (minus the Tyler tidbits) is how I began my essay for English. Ms. Mitchell told us to write about something we know or care about or don't quite understand. Ez was my first choice since he fits all three. I finished the thing in one sitting. The words flowed like spring water.

OCTOBER 15
Hey Dee,

Today Ms. Mitchell asked to see me after class. OMG. What have I done now??? I was ready for a lecture on . . . what? I didn't know.

"Do you know why I've asked to see you?" she said with an expression I couldn't read.

"No, Ms. Mitchell, I don't."

"Jennifer," she said, "I think you have written a very fine essay, and you should consider expanding it into a term paper on growing up with your brother, Ezra." Smiling broadly, she declared my paper A+ material. How about that? *A+ material.* Hmmm! Didn't see that one coming.

Truth is, I really liked the assignment and missed it when it was over. That's when I decided to sit down every day and write myself a keep-out, private, confidential, just-for-me, Jennifer Lee Lauler, letter. And that's how Dee was born. Dee, my secret diary about me and life with Ezra, my wacky, exasperating, infuriating, positively amazing, younger brother.

OCTOBER 16
Dear Dee,

His last name is Tomsen. Tyler Tomsen, a name that belongs on a marquee.

OCTOBER 17
Dear Dee,

Tryouts for *My Fair Lady* begin next week, and Zoe and I decided to go for it. I know I'm a long shot, but last night I looked at myself in the mirror and the verdict was close to . . . not bad. You might even say, if you're generous, I'm on the verge of attractive. Auburn hair curls around my chin and I'm beginning to look OK.

I don't look fifteen yet but I can pass for fourteen and three-quarters. Mom says I'm becoming a lovely girl with my most beautiful leaves yet to unfold. WHATEVER. I'm so tired of having to wait for some grand spring awakening. I want to look like

Serena Spencer now, yesterday, or at least by tryout time. Guess Ez isn't the only one genetically opposed to waiting.

I'll bet my bottom baby-sitting dollar Serena Spencer never had to wait for her leaves to unfold. I'm sure from day one she sprang fully formed and hourglass perfect. Serena doesn't walk; she glides. Her skin is silken and she thinks "acne" is a political action group.

OCTOBER 18
Dear Dee,

Zoe said she heard Serena Spencer is trying out for *My Fair Lady*. Awesome! Guess I'll be a potted plant.

Ms. Fox is looking for strong voices and a natural stage presence. I'll be lucky if I AM a potted plant.

OCTOBER 19
Hi Dee,

Tonight the SCOOP editorial board is meeting at our house. Zoe and Samantha no longer wince when Ezra bursts into the room blasting commercials about urinary leakage. And diarrhea. But the SCOOP kids haven't been initiated yet and I'm not exactly in a hurry for this inevitable moment. "Enablex, Miralax, Dulcolax, Levitra, Viagra!" One time may be cute, but 100 might be teen abuse. I hate it when kids try to hide a snicker or put on a sugar-coated grin. I make lame jokes just to keep them laughing . . . at anything but Ezra.

It's like the party we had in sixth grade. Ez didn't like his clothes anymore, so he graced us with his adorable self wearing only shoes. Back then kids didn't hide how freaked they were. They gawked at him like he was a train wreck or something. Yeah, I know, that was then and this is now, but I still hold my breath when friends come over. I never know when he'll blurt out "you have bad breath" or "too many zits," or just sit in a corner belching.

Mom said she'd take Ezra to the mall before the SCOOPs arrive. She knows every thought in my head even when I fake it. With her hand on the door, she turned and said, "You know, Jen, chances are we'll be back before your friends leave. Remember, we can't stay away forever."

OCTOBER 20
Hi Dee,

I feel slightly ill whenever I think about what Mom said yesterday. Sure I wanted Ezra out of my life last night, but last night is not the same as forever. Is it? I love my brother and I'd go to the moon for him. But there are times I wish he would disappear for a month or two or four. Does that make me a witch or something?

Before the meeting was over, Ez *did* come home and he was perfectly fine. Sure, he poked his head in the dining room, and said "hi" to the floor. Yeah, he knocked over a flower vase while trying to wave hello. But hey, there was no water in the vase and it was no big deal. No need to wish he were parked on Mars. Wish I could be more like Mom . . . don't know how she does it.

After all the SCOOPs left, I stood by Ez's door and watched him gently breathing, drifting off to sleep. His butterscotch curls crowned his head, his face was pink, and I swear, he looked like an angel.

"You're beautiful, Ez," I whispered.

OCTOBER 21

Dear Dee,

Tyler asked me for our homework assignment in science. It was on hormones. Can you believe?

OCTOBER 22

Hi Dee,

While I was searching in drawers for a *My Fair Lady* CD, I found photos of Ezra and me in the garden when we were little. When my heart began racing, I remembered the picture was from *that* day. I shoved the thing deep in the drawer, hoping that's where the memory would stay. Ha!

OCTOBER 23

Hi Dee,

Dad was grumpy and tired at dinner tonight, nothing like the charming talk-a-thon all my friends go gaga over. As he bent down to pick up his napkin, I noticed a new patch of silver hair and a few more lines around his eyes. The small scar above his brow has almost faded, except when he rubs it like a worry bead. Like tonight when he was prickly and got on Ez's case.

"Sit up straight, Ezra, and look me in the eye, and for once sit at the table 'til everyone's done."

"I *am* sitting straight in my chair," Ez shouts in a gravelly voice. "I *am* sitting straight. My back is straight in my chair. I want you to leave me alone. Leave me alone, please."

"But I don't want you to *want* to be alone," Dad said softly.

Mom served Dad's favorite soup and eased the tension with sprinkles of stardust. She can do that like nobody I know. Good thing. We have a whole lot of tension that needs a whole lot of stardust. I love to watch her hands forever moving . . . stirring the soup, pouring coffee, fingers dancing. There she was with her quiet smile and turquoise eyes. Her auburn hair is darker than mine but she still wears it to her shoulders. My mom moves like a ballerina and touches our lives with magic.

While Mom and Dad were talking politics, Ez left the table clutching his Nintendo. Dad forgot to be mad and wanted to chat. He asked me about school and Zoe and *My Fair Lady* tryouts. I told him Zoe was thinking about running for class president.

"And if she does, I'll be her campaign manager," I crowed.

"Why isn't my Jenny Jen running for class president?" he asked, taking my hand in his.

"Because of course I would win without even trying," I said with mock conceit.

"Oh, so you're stepping aside to let others take the lead," Dad said with a chuckle.

"You got it," I said.

And he thinks I'm kidding.

OCTOBER 24
Dear Dee,

If I do get a part in *My Fair Lady,* which I'm not counting on, but if I do, which I won't, either Mom or Dad will be missing at curtain time. Mom says taking Ez to social events is like an advertisement for Pepto Bismol. When Ezra stages one of his numbers in public, Dad fumes and Mom and I look for the nearest manhole. So what do we do instead? We quarantine ourselves at home like we are radioactive or something. When we do go somewhere special, one of us stays home with Ez while the other two go it alone. So we're one happy, splintered family. Today Ezra went bonkers in a restaurant because the booth he thought was his was already taken. When people began shooting glances (or worse yet, calling for the manager), we hightailed it home and stared at yesterday's spaghetti with no sauce.

Sometimes I think Ezra can control his tantrums. Sometimes I think we're too easy on him. Dad does lay down the law, but often overdoes it. Mom goes to the other extreme trying to make up for Dad. Whether or not Ez can control his tantrums, I know for sure anyone with a kid in *My Fair Lady* will be in the audience shouting bravo, stomping their feet in a standing O. And I'll be scanning the theater, looking for Mom *or* Dad, wondering which one won't be there. Yeah, I know there are greater tragedies in the universe, but sometimes I forget to remember what they are.

OCTOBER 25
Hey Dee,

Zoe decided to run for class president. And I will be the best campaign manager Washington has ever seen. Sorry Dad.

OCTOBER 26
Dear Dee,

Ardath Savage caught me at lunch today. Ardath Savage is wide and built like an overstuffed chair. She actually asked me if my parents are divorced. Can you believe it? What business is it of hers? Do I ask her about her parents' love life? Guess she noticed Mom and Dad are rarely together for stuff at school. I didn't explain.

Sure, everyone at school knows about Ezra. You don't have to be a rocket scientist to figure it out. But I don't talk about him to anyone but Zoe, who's almost like a sister, so Ez is almost like her brother. Zoe's known Ezra all his life and has seen him grow inch by slow inch. But I rarely talk about him even to her. She doesn't ask and I don't tell. If I were to bare my soul about Ez, I'd worry she might turn against him or think less of me or say something about him I couldn't forgive. So I stay silent.

OCTOBER 27
Hi Dee,

I've designed a poster for Zoe's campaign:

VOTE FOR ZOE MEADER

A GREAT FRIEND . . . A GREAT LEADER

OCTOBER 28
Hey Dee,

I showed Dad the Zoe poster. He said, "How about this slogan?"

VOTE FOR JENNIFER LAULER

A WINNER AND A SCHOLAR

The man never gives up.

OCTOBER 29

Dear Dee,

Zoe and I have been singing duets to get up to speed for tryouts. We are a super team and if I may say so myself, I think we're getting close to actually being almost good.

Zoe says she wishes there were a part we could sing together. So do I. Zoe is tall and slim. I'm shorter and rounder. Apart from that, we both have the same sandy hair and everyone thinks we're sisters.

Truth is we were BFFs even before we were born. Our moms were moms-in-waiting together, so we were hanging out when we were in our mommas' bellies. We've been buddies since preschool and it would be perfect if we could go to the same college . . . that is *if* I can let myself leave home. Between you and me, I'd love to go away to college, but I'd probably bounce myself right back to 22 Elm, Evanston, IL.

OCTOBER 30

Hey Dee,

You've never seen a collection of more spastic kids in your life. At tryouts today everyone was bouncing like jumping jacks, including yours truly. The guys were almost blasé by comparison. Not sure why. Maybe they're just better at covering nervous with cool. Zoe and I had a giggle fit like we used to in first grade. She was sure she lost a few votes because of it. I was sure kids were thinking, "Jenny's brother isn't the only SPAZ in the family." WHATEVER.

OCTOBER 31

Hi Dee,

Zoe and I made the first cut. So did Tyler. So did Serena Spencer. Natch.

NOVEMBER: TALKING TURKEY

NOVEMBER 2

Dear Dee,

I hope both Zoe and I make it to the finals, but if one of us has to be cut, I'd rather it be me. If that sounds weird, it's only because it is. I've always been that way. I don't like envying a friend, but I really get spooked if she envies me. It's not like I'm a martyr or anything, and I'm no stranger to competition. It's just that people can get nasty when you're the chosen one, the gifted one, the one who walks away with the gold. It's a messy business getting what others want. If you beat out your BFF, you win but she feels bad . . . so it's a slightly tarnished victory. Not sure everyone else feels this way, though.

NOVEMBER 3

Dear Dee,

I pulled the photo out from hiding and once again relived *that* day. It happened when Ez was four and I was seven.

The day is pleasant and bright. It's spring. Ez and I are playing together in the garden. I'm counting tulips; he's lining up stones. While smiling at our lilacs, I turn and glance to my side. OMG!!! I can't find Ezra. My four-year-old brother with garbled speech, who trusts pebbles more than people, who can get lost standing still, has disappeared, is missing . . . is absolutely gone.

I call his name 'til my throat is on fire. I holler, I scream, I circle the yard like a crazy loon. "Where are you, Ezra? Please answer me. Are you lost in the woods or snatched up by a bear?" I'm sick to my stomach and afraid to tell Mom. The longer I wait the worse it gets. A weird thought pops into my head. If Ezra were truly taken from us, would Mom and Dad want him back? I'd heard about animals that neglect their young if they're sick or lame or different from the rest. Would that happen to my little brother?

I run into the house screaming, "Ezra is gone. Ezra isn't here. I can't find Ezra."

Mom darts out of the house shouting a ton of questions. How long was he gone, where was he last seen, where was I before he disappeared? Every "I don't know" does me in. Let's face it; it's all my fault.

We search the woods. We scour the neighborhood. We call his name 'til it echoes through the trees.

EZZRRAAAA, Ezzrraaaa.

Mom calls Dad at the store. He's home in a heartbeat. They run through the neighborhood like racehorses. "Have you seen a four-year-old boy in overalls and a red plaid shirt?" they scream at no one, everyone.

We give up and call the cops. Oh, how I hope they'll never come. If police come to our house, of course they'd be coming for me.

"You're the one responsible for your brother's disappearance," they'd scold, "and you must go to prison for the rest of your life." Ezra will be lost, I'll be in prison, and Mom and Dad won't visit because it's all my fault. I promise myself *I'll never again be sassy or rude or nasty if only my brother will come back home.* I barf on a rosebush. Nobody notices. Nobody cares.

After a long and desperate search, a dazed little boy appears in the garden. Is it only a dream? Ezra had wandered off to a neighbor's shed, where he spent hours lining up nuts and bolts, happy to be in a people-less world. Had Mr. Norton not shown him home, Ezra would still be there. *Thank you, thank you, thank you Mr. Norton for bringing my little brother back home! Thank you—whoever—for not sending me to jail.*

After *that* day, I never felt like a kid again. The carefree lollipop days I once took for granted were replaced with the vigil of a mother hen. Ever since then, an invisible cord connects Ezra and me. As though we're attached by an expandable leash, I feel his tug when he wanders too far and I constantly wonder, where is he? Is he safe? Who's he with? Are they kind? Distances between us are scary, the cord between us tightens.

NOVEMBER 4
Dear Dee,

Zoe is in third place for class president. Brad Neuworth is the front-runner. No surprise. He's worked for kids in Darfur, and will probably end up in the White House. He's kind of cute but I wish he were taller than me.

Tyler isn't running. He's walking. So looks aren't everything, Prince Tyler.

NOVEMBER 5

Dee,

My straw poll says Zoe is slipping below third place. I'm sure it's my fault. Mom says I blame myself for every second thing that goes wrong. "Are you responsible for the Iraq war?" she asks. "Only Afghanistan," I say.

Time for new posters. How's this, Dee?

VOTE FOR ZOE, SHE'S THE ONE

CHARACTER, IDEAS, AND JOBS WELL DONE

NOVEMBER 6

Hey Dee,

Tyler says he's going to be the next class president.

Give me a break!

NOVEMBER 7

Hi Dee,

Mom and I went clothes shopping today. A full afternoon with her alone! Cool, cool, crazy cool! No therapists, no doctors, and NO EZRA. I love to hang out with Dad, too. He always has a fascinating story to tell and tell and tell. And Dad's right out there. His moods are painted in bright colors; even Ez can't miss them. Mom's are more subtle. Her moods are pastel but I can read them with my eyes shut. Ditto her with mine. Today we were both electric blue. Matched the sweaters we bought for fall.

Dear Dee,

Ezra's been mainstreamed in Roosevelt's K–5 public school. My middle school is connected to his by a long hall that bridges the two. Today Samantha and I cut through Ez's school on the way to ours. Dodging kids racing to class as the last bell rings, I suddenly see a humongous girl pinning Ezra to the wall. His eyes are popping, he's grunting and straining to pry himself free. This behemoth is caging him with her tree trunk arms and locking his feet with her heavy boots. I throw down my books and fly over to take that witch on. Even though she's gigantic, she darts away so fast I can't catch up. Ez somehow manages to get it together to find his class, his first order of business, no matter the crisis.

I ask every kid in the hall if they know who that pit bull is. I discover her name is Francine and she is in eighth grade. Can you believe? Ez is three years younger and lives with problems he didn't exactly choose. But she doesn't care; she even makes everything worse. Why? What makes people want to pick on innocent kids? Do they get their kicks from making others squirm? Can't get my mind around this one, Dee.

My work at SCOOP lets me get kids out of class for interviews. I use my reporter's privilege to pull Pit Bull into the hall. Francine comes out and I let her have it. I tell her I am Ezra's sister and proud of it. "I hope you're really thrilled with yourself for being cruel to kids who are younger and smaller and less able to stick up for themselves," I said. I scream with a fury I never knew I had. I get in her face and give her a piece of my mind. She thinks I'm going to pummel her. I don't, of course. I look straight into her hard-bitten face and say "if I ever catch you bullying my brother again, I'll splash it all over the front page of SCOOP and then I will send it to the city newspapers, and put it online. I'm sure you'll make your parents proud."

After I took on that Pit Bull, I walked by Ez's class to see how he was doing. He was completely focused on his reading, his index finger following each line. Ezra was totally immersed in the day's assignment, his whole body leaning into the task. I stood there a while, absolutely blown away by my remarkable brother, bravely soldiering on. As I watched him with ballooning pride, the invisible cord twitched, and he noticed me standing at the door. His face lit up. He waved and his eyes smiled. It was one of those magical Ezra-Jenny moments.

NOVEMBER 9
Hey Dee,

Talked to Brad Neuworth, future lawyer, and future class president, about doing an exposé on bullying. He loved the idea. "When do we begin?" he asked.

"Yesterday," I said.

NOVEMBER 10
Dear Dee,

Zoe told me that the neighborhood wingnut is a loner. Yes, Ez, too, looks at the wall . . . but what a screaming world of difference.

NOVEMBER 11
Dear Dee,

Today I was shooting basketballs and Ez was keeping score. Tyler, Mr. Drop Dead Gorgeous, swaggered over to tell me I should spend more time working on my arc. "Anything less than an hour a day is just a drop in the bucket," he declared.

"It's not a bucket," Ezra yelled. "It's a basket. We're throwing the ball into a basket not a bucket."

"Oh I am so very, very sorry, Ezra," Tyler says, over-enunciating each word.

He's a bit too snide for my taste and I no longer think he's drop-dead gorgeous.

NOVEMBER 12
Dear Dee,

For the past few weeks, I've been thinking about a summer program in Indiana for young journalists that Ms. Mitchell recommended. I won't tell Mom and Dad because I know they'll make me apply. How can I go away for two full months with Francine *and* the wingnut lurking in the shadows? The invisible cord forever tightens. When you think about it, Dee, I'm not only Ezra's sister; I am his protector, his defender, his best and only friend. How can I disappear for eight long weeks when I am literally my brother's keeper?

But going to Indiana would be a giant step toward becoming a first rate, top-notch reporter.

"Breaking News" . . . by Jennifer Lee Lauler!

How cool is that?

NOVEMBER 13
Dear Dee,

Decided not to tell Mom and Dad about Francine. It would only upset them. They'd tell the school, people would talk, rumors would fly, and in the end nothing would happen anyway. Well . . . I will make something happen! Just you wait!

NOVEMBER 14

Dear Dee,

Ez is home with a bad cold, and his speech is returning to its old ways. Reminds me of when I used to play speech school with him and Mom.

After the anguish of *that* day, I was haunted by the thought of my brother being lost and unable to speak his name. Though Ez had trouble remembering people's names, he could easily label *things* and could say a ton of words. But pronunciation was his biggest hang-up. He'd drop consonants, especially those at the beginning or end of a word. "I go pwe koo" (I go to pre-school), he'd say, or "I onn eep wahs nie" (I couldn't sleep last night). Because we were everyday buddies, I could understand him completely. Most of the time Mom and Dad could, too, but every once in a while they'd ask me to explain.

"Translating 'Ezra speak' is in no way helpful," Ms. Livingston, his therapist said. "It only reinforces immature speech that no one else understands." Our work was cut out for us. Like Henry Higgins with Eliza Doolittle, Mom and I were determined to teach Ezra "proper" English. I borrowed some of Ms. Livingston's worn out flash cards, matched words to pictures, exaggerated the correct sounds, and asked Ez to repeat, repeat, repeat. Every freaking day, Mom and I chanted "lettuce leaves, lettuce leaves" until we were blue in the face. Then one day, without warning, Ez announced, "Lettuce leaves are near the school."

"I think he's got it," we cheered. "We think he's got it. The rain in Spain stays mainly in the plain."

Next we moved to pronouns . . . but that's another story.

NOVEMBER 15
Dear Dee,

Zoe is pulling up in the polls. I think she has a real chance. During the campaign, I was thinking back to third grade when we spent the whole summer together and bought each other friendship rings. As we get older, and in my case rounder, we have the rings made larger. We promise to be bridesmaids at each other's weddings and name our daughters after each other. If Zoe wins this election, I think I will be just as happy as she is. What do you think of that, Dad?

NOVEMBER 16
Dear Dee,

It used to be a royal pain for Ezra when he had to shuttle back and forth between class and his locker at school. He'd pick the wrong book, misplace another, and end up in blinking confusion. Dad thought it would be better to keep his belongings in a backpack so his stuff would be literally on his back. Next day, he brought home a neat backpack right off Lauler's shelves. The plan spared Ez frequent trips to his locker, but not the constant teasing from other kids. "There goes the hunchback of Notre Dame," they'd shout. "Hey, look. Think that turtle can fit in his shell?"

Mostly harmless teasing, but one more thing Ez doesn't exactly need.

But today someone grabs a pair of scissors and cuts a huge hole in his backpack lying on the lunchroom floor. When Ez tries to hoist the thing on his shoulders, all its contents spill out. Pens scatter, books fly, and notebooks get smeared with lunchroom gunk. Ez has a GIANT meltdown, smack in the middle of the cafeteria. Some kids jeer and laugh their heads off; others stand there doing absolutely nothing. Soon he's hustled off to the school counselor who calls me out of class to settle him down. They used to call Mom whenever he would have a tantrum. But now he only calms down if I show up.

I showed up, but he didn't calm down.

I'm pretty sure this is Francine's handiwork, but I don't have proof. YET. No one will say what they saw. It seems like they're too afraid to talk. Why do I believe it's Pit Bull's doing? It has all the markings of her brand of nastiness . . . as cruel as she is sneaky.

NOVEMBER 17
Dear Dee,

The second round of tryouts is in a few days. Not sure I'll make the cut. I'll be happy to be a fern.

NOVEMBER 18
Dear Dee,

Everyone is talking about rock stars and rappers and all the rest. I listen. I have things to say and can talk about that stuff as well as the best of them. But sometimes my mind wanders. Only a few days ago, I wanted to pummel a girl who was picking on my brother. Things like that don't disappear or leave me worry-free like your typical all-American teen. I think about getting even or what might happen to Ez the next time and the time after that. I live in a silent world of worries my friends don't have. Sure, I too want to look good, have zit-free skin and a cute boyfriend. But sometimes I feel there's a gaping distance between them and me. It's like I am two different Jennys. One everyone knows, one nobody knows. That sometimes makes me feel alone, standing on the margins, not really fitting in. When push comes to shove, I am different from the others. Even Zoe sometimes. She worries about the size of her hips; I worry about my brother playing in traffic. When they wig out over being grounded for one stupid night, I have trouble feeling sorry for them. I go through the motions. Try to look like I care. But I don't. Guess they'll soon see through my charade. Frankly, I'd rather act on a real stage. Like in *My Fair Lady* with the rain in Spain.

NOVEMBER 19
Dear Dee,

It's getting closer. The second round of tryouts begins tomorrow. I've been trilling like a songbird.

NOVEMBER 20
Dear Dee,

You'd think this round of tryouts would be less nutzoid. It wasn't. The stakes are even higher now. Kids who were friends for life are looking at each other suspiciously. "There goes Chloe, she's had voice lessons. There's Rachel, her mom was a professional singer, not fair." And, of course, "there goes Serena Spencer who doesn't have to do anything but be . . . Serena Spencer."

While girls were hitting the high notes, I was scanning Foxy's expression. She tried to keep a straight face, but when a smile broke through you knew that kid made the cut. When I was singing, I didn't see a single flicker of approval, not even around the edges. Zoe said she thought Foxy really liked her voice. Forget what I said about envy. I wish she had liked mine, too.

NOVEMBER 21
Dear Dee,

At lunch today, Megan Morrison said she heard about our SCOOP project on bullying and was eager to join. Megan doesn't write for SCOOP, so I wondered what sparked her interest. I wanted to come right out and ask, but I didn't. I've learned to wait rather than push my way in like Ardath Savage, that tactless, over-stuffed eighth grader.

Megan has a cheerleader's cuteness, and could easily make the squad. Yesterday I saw her talking to Cynthia Grey, who usually sits alone wishing someone would notice her. I talk to Cynthia, too, but never thought anyone else cared. Megan came to Roosevelt this year from a different school. Don't know why. Whatever the reasons, I'm glad she wants to work on the project, because I want to work with Megan.

NOVEMBER 22
Hey Dee,

Zoe, Samantha, and I made the cut. So did Tyler. So did Serena Spencer.

NOVEMBER 23
Dear Dee,

Tyler and I were hanging out after tryouts today and I couldn't think of a thing to say. I stood there mute, grasping for something, anything, but my brain had turned to tofu. Not sure why. Think it has to do with baskets vs. buckets.

Brad would never act like such a jerk.

NOVEMBER 24

Hey Dee,

Met with Megan and Brad for a project-planning session before Thanksgiving break. Each of us has our assigned beats and I'm really pumped about this project. Megan is psyched, too. Still don't know why. The reporter in me sniffs a backstory. Whatever it is, I like Megan Morrison. Can't wait for our next SCOOP meeting.

NOVEMBER 25

Dear Dee,

The leaves are falling and there's a crispness to the air. I love this time of year, especially when we have Thanksgiving at home. I love the mingled scents of food and holiday flowers . . . I love having cousins and both sets of Grands gather around our table. And I love Gram's absolutely to-die-for chocolate cake.

This morning Mom asked me to run a few errands for her. So Ez and I rode our bikes to pick up a few "forgottens" for tomorrow's dinner. As soon as we hit the supermarket, Ezra makes a beeline for the junk food, fills his cart with potato chips and pretzels, and accidentally spills popcorn across the floor. I place everything back on the shelves, clean up the mess, and wonder if this trip is really necessary.

Ezra begins blinking and flapping his hands. Lately he can do short jaunts to the supermarket without melting down. But I should have known. The colors, the clatter, the hordes of Thanksgiving shoppers overwhelm him. He begins grabbing videos from their stacks, laughing his honk of a laugh, sounding like the horn of an antique car.

Slowly people start moving away, turning their backs, pretending not to notice. An old woman with a beak nose wheels around, *tsk tsks*, and throws darts with her eyes. A large hulk of a man bends down, stands nose to nose with poor Ez and lectures him on his "outrageous" behavior.

I usually shut down when this sort of stuff happens. But for some reason today was different. I walked right up to that man, looked him in the eye and said, "My brother has autism, and he's doing the best he can. Scoldings from strangers only make matters worse."

The man looked startled, lowered his head, and mumbled, "I'm sorry."

Wow! That was a first.

NOVEMBER 26
Dear Dee,

Today was turkey day. I helped Mom do the trimmings, set the table, and arrange the flowers. As she put the turkey in the oven, Mom called us kids to say goodbye to "Timothy," the name she gave our twenty-pound bird. Ezra was not at all charmed by this naming game. "Turkeys don't have names," he protested. "Turkeys aren't people and we don't give them names, Jen." Again, I should have known. Even when we were little, Ez could never understand "make believe." He'd scream at the top of his lungs, "teddy bears can't talk and wooden dolls can't walk!" In Ezra's world there is no room for pretend, no place for Santa Claus or leprechauns or four-leaf clovers. He's like Sergeant Friday, from an old TV series Dad likes to quote: "Just the facts, ma'am, just the facts." Though I've always known this about my brother, once in a while I forget and hope that maybe *this* time he'll discover the joys of fun and play with me.

Gram and Gramps Wilson and Granny and Grandpa Lauler arrived with tons of gifts for us grandkids. Ez grabbed his present, ripped off the wrapping paper, and found new videos to watch later. Mom told him to sit at the table until dinner was finished. But the moment dinner was over he leapt from the table, planted himself in front of the TV and had a full throttle "ad spaz." He offered an endless recitation of every wacko commercial that ever hit the talking screen: "ActivOn, Apply Directly Where It Hurts, ActivOn, Geico, ActivOn, Aricept, ActivOn . . . "

When we joined him in the TV room for a string of football games, all was calm until Ez began changing channels in the middle of a play. Grandpa Lauler exploded. "That boy is thoroughly spoiled, you know that, George, don't you? You and Martha continue to ask so little of him, of course he doesn't act his age. If you want him to grow up, you've got to show him what's expected of a boy who's almost twelve *and* you've got to hold him to it."

Dad didn't answer, just quietly changed the channel back to the game. It wasn't long before Ez grabbed the remote and channel-surfed again. Grandpa bolted out of the TV room and stormed upstairs shouting, "That's the last straw!" "We have more straws," Ez explains. "We have more straws in the kitchen." No one split their sides laughing. Dad followed Grandpa to the study and the two growled at each other like a pair of grizzlies. Can you believe all this started because Grandpa and Dad wanted to watch a stupid game which neither of them got to see? And they say Ezra should act *his* age?

Mom and Gram Wilson were clearing the table while eavesdropping on the ruckus upstairs. "What's going on up there, Jenny?" Gram asked. I didn't dodge the question even though I knew it would open up a can of worms. "Grandpa got mad and said that Ezra is overindulged and under-disciplined," I said.

"I think Grandpa is right about that," Gram said, raising her eyebrows, looking in Mom's direction. That's when it hit the fan. Mom doesn't usually get into back-and-forth bickering, but this time she was furious.

"We have lived with our son for over eleven years, mother," she said, "and we know well what is possible and what is not. He's come a long way in these last few years and we're helping him every way we know how." Her voice was steady but her eyes were moist.

NOVEMBER 27
Dear Dee,

After everyone left last night, I could hear Mom and Dad arguing about Ezra again. Even though Dad was ticked off with Grandpa, he actually agrees with what he said. Dad honestly believes that Ezra could behave if only firm limits were set and reasonable rules were respected. I've heard that one over and over but this time it gave me the widgets. Dad's growing more impatient with Ezra and points the finger at Mom. "You treat him like a baby. He's almost twelve now, Martha, we need to prepare him for adulthood and now is not too soon." That's Dad's constant mantra, always reminding Mom of Ezra's age, like she doesn't know when the kid was born.

Since this "discussion" was going on in the kitchen, I decided to go downstairs and get my third piece of chocolate cake. With my heart racing, I took a big breath, walked into the breakfast room, and put myself smack down in the middle, Mom on one side, Dad on the other. I tried some kitchen diplomacy.

"Listen up," I said. "Because Mom has the patience of a saint, she rarely gets mad at Ezra. But Dad and I have short fuses so we want to believe he melts down on purpose. Then we feel we have a right to be mad." Turning up the volume, I said, "Forcing him to behave really doesn't work, Dad. When he knows we're angry, his tantrums get worse and the whole thing spirals out of control." Mom looked at me with that admiring "how did you get so smart so soon" look. Dad listened with a trace of chagrin.

Chagrin is Ms. Mitchell's favorite word.

They went upstairs together, but the "discussion" wasn't over . . . no way. As I write this tonight, Dee, I can hear their voices rising again. Disciplining Ezra has always been a sore point between them, but lately things are getting worse. Something is weird between them. Can't put my finger on it, but they're like two strangers sitting in a bus. They talk but they don't really say anything. Maybe it's all in my head. Maybe not.

So what do I do about this one, Dee? Compare notes with my brother? ActivOn, Apply Directly Where It Hurts, ActivOn, Apply Directly Where It Hurts.

NOVEMBER 28
Dear Dee,

Today's Dad's busiest day at the store, and I thought I'd stop by and check things out. When I arrived, Dad was talking up an awesome tote bag to a customer. He looked fully recovered from yesterday's spat. His face brightened when he saw me, and he proudly introduced me to Aviva, the new store manager. Aviva is young and glamorous and looks like a model. She has flaming red hair, seriously white teeth, and a camera-ready smile. Uh oh, what do we have brewing here? Stay tuned.

NOVEMBER 29
Dear Dee,

Megan texted me today asking if I wanted to meet at the mall for Christmas shopping. Since Zoe and I shop every Thanksgiving weekend, I suggested we all go together. When I called Zoe, she said in an un-Zoe-like tone, "I have other plans." Between you and me, I wanted Megan and me to go alone. She's becoming a special friend unlike any other. My text read, "Meg c u @ mall in 30 secs. cn't wt!"

LATER
Zoe asked about how it went today shopping with Megan. I talked about the crowds, what I bought, and who I met. I told her everything she didn't want to know and nothing she did. Zoe will always be my friend. But I really like hanging with Megan, too. Does having a new friend mean having to give up an old one?

Megan and I have big plans for our SCOOP story and we're eager to get the thing rolling. I gently asked if she knew anyone who'd been targeted by a bully. She was about to say something, paused, then changed her mind. I backed off. Now I will wait 'til the time is right. Listen up, Ardath Savage, you who dared ask if my parents were divorced. Take a lesson from me . . . you prying, snoopy buttinsky.

NOVEMBER 30
Dear Dee,

I met with Mr. Harrington to get permission for the series on bullying. Harris Harrington III, our school principal, is really a trip! Harris Harrington III wears three-piece suits, a crooked hairpiece, and is forever sniff, sniff, sniffing like he smells a skunk. Harris Harrington III talks without moving his lips and ends his sentences with "if you will" or "so to speak."

After I told him about the article on bullying, he rose from his chair, stretched to his full height and said, "The idea for your project is a fine one, Jennifer"—it's always bad news when adults call me Jennifer—"but I want to give it careful consideration before I give you the green light to print, so to speak. I must consult my faculty and the parent organization so I can take the pulse of the larger Roosevelt community, so to speak. I'll get back to you as soon as we've reached a consensus, if you will. I will consult with Mr. Alter who will advise your SCOOP project and keep me abreast of its progress, if you will."

LATER
More, Dee,

OMG. Why do I have to wait for everything I can't wait for? A part in *My Fair Lady,* "my most beautiful leaves to unfold," and a nod from "if you will."

When I left HH III's office, Brad was waiting to hear the final verdict. I told him Harris Harrington the Too Many didn't say yes. He didn't say no. He did say, "We'll have to wait and see."

Forever on a Wait List: A Teen's Memoir, by Jennifer Lee Lauler.

Got an email from Brad.

> *Jen,*
>
> *How about going ahead w/out HH, The 2 Many? Then we'll have a head start before he gives a thumbs-up, so to speak.*
>
> *Eager in Evanston*

I wrote him back:

> *Dear Eager,*
>
> *I've already started work on the project. I do believe you've been SCOOP-ed, so to speak. I want to go ahead*

with the story even if HH says no through his nose. If he tries to silence us, we'll make him part of the story. Can you see it now? "Principal Harris Harrington III obstructs student exposé on school bullying." Be my guest, HH, The Too Many, if you will.

Evil in Evanston

Brad wrote:

Dear Evil,

So you think I've been SCOOP-ed, do ya? Well, for some time now, I've been talking to guys from other schools and they've served up the best poop for SCOOP. How do you like them apples, Ms. Chief Correspondent?

Me:

OK, Gonzo. You are the best pooper scooper in Evanston. Hey, by the way, what do you do with the poop you scoop?

Andrea Mitchell, reporting

Brad:

Dump it on Harris Harrington's desk . . . he can sniff, sniff, sniff, 'til the cows come home.

Me:

LOL. You've made my day.

DECEMBER: WISHING FOR WILLY

DECEMBER 1
Dear Dee,

Told Mom and Dad about the project.

They told me about the writing program in Indiana . . . they heard about it at a PTO meeting. Wow!!! How do they always know what I want even when I think it's a secret?

DECEMBER 2
Hey Dee,

When I was teaching little Ez to speak clearly, I thought I'd be a speech therapist. When I was helping him avoid meltdowns, I was sure I'd be a psychotherapist. But if this SCOOP exposé ever sees the light of day, I'll want nothing more than to be a journalist.

DECEMBER 3
Dear Dee,

Foxy will finally announce the casting for *My Fair Lady* this week. I'm not even sure I'll be a fern.

DECEMBER 4

Dear Dee,

At night Mom and Dad have hushed discussions that sound like an ongoing fight. And at dinner they are far too polite with each other. Too many "pleases" and "thank yous," like they're talking to a clerk at a department store. Even when they're both home, the house is weirdly quiet. Funny how silence can sometimes seem louder than a scream.

DECEMBER 5

Dear Dee,

Went to Lauler's today. Aviva wasn't there. Dad wasn't either. Went to the café. They were both there. Together. She was flashing her *Cover Girl* smile. Dad seemed oblivious. I think. Women are always flirting with my handsome dad and he doesn't really notice. But this Aviva person may be another story.

DECEMBER 7

Dear Dee,

An election is coming up and Mom and Dad are on the same page, laugh at the same jokes, and cheer for the same candidates. Ez asked if a lame duck president is one with a broken webbed foot. "This one is," Dad said. Mom thought that was hilarious. Things are more upbeat between them.

Don't know what I'd do without you, Dee. I can sort out stuff, keep things between us, and always feel about 50 lbs. lighter.

DECEMBER 8

Dear Dee,

Well, I don't have to be a potted plant or a fern. Foxy finally announced the casting for *My Fair Lady* today. Neither Zoe nor I got a leading role. But neither did Serena Spencer. Tyler was cast as Henry Higgins even though he sings off key!

Zoe and I were chosen for the servants' chorus. We're trying not to take it personally. At least we were chosen; lots of kids weren't, and we'll have a ton of fun at rehearsals. Ashley Sorenson will play Eliza Doolittle. She will be fantastic. She'll be a showstopper in the scene where Eliza goes to the racetrack to show off her "proper" English only to shock the proper Brits by slipping into her native Cockney. The play is scheduled for early spring. Can't wait!!!

Wonder which one will be missing on opening night . . . Mom or Dad?

DECEMBER 9
Dear Dee,

Punching Ezra's backpack with both her fists, Francine shouts, "Sorry about your hunchback, Notre Dame." Neither Ez nor I were bothered. Either she's lightened up or we have.

DECEMBER 10
Hey Dee,

Megan and I spend lots of time together working on the project. She sits at our lunch table every day and Zoe is more than slightly wigged over it. Zoe's still with us at lunch, but signs of her being ticked are none too subtle.

Why does life have to be such a balancing act, Dee? If summer camp, no Ezra. If Megan, no Zoe. If HH, no exposé. If you can name one freaking thing that's easy in life, would you shoot me an email??

DECEMBER 11
Dear Dee,

At rehearsal today Zoe hung out with Ashley Sorenson whenever she had the chance. See what I mean? I knew it, I knew it, I knew it. Since Megan has become my friend, Zoe wants to find a new friend of her own. Not sure where this will lead.

DECEMBER 12
Dear Dee,

Megan has been spending every free minute on the exposé, way beyond the call of duty. Why?

DECEMBER 13
Hey Dee,

Tyler may be drop dead gorgeous but Brad is much more appealing. This guy is the real deal, not just a walking Adonis. If our school burst into flames, Tyler would run for his life. Brad would stop to take others with him.

DECEMBER 14
Hi Dee,

Tyler and Serena are an item. Obviously!

DECEMBER 15
Dear Dee,

Megan was poring over piles of documents for the project and suddenly I found myself saying, "You really care about this exposé, don't you, Meg?" She nodded. I wanted her to say more.

She didn't. "What triggered your interest in this project?" I finally asked.

Slowly she began talking. She said her dad, who was the person she most admired in the world, was a prominent human rights lawyer who served victims of hate crimes in the U.S. and other countries across the globe. He risked his life in countries ravaged by civil wars, helping those who suffered unimaginable atrocities. Looking down at her hands clutching a pencil, she said, "Two years ago, he lost his life on one of those missions. Though my dad will never again be with us," she said, "at least I can keep his work alive. He'd be happy to see me working on this exposé. I'm doing it for him but also for me. So yeah," she said with a foggy gaze, "now you know the story behind my interest in the project."

I thought I once knew the meaning of "kindred spirit." I didn't until today. Megan will always be my friend.

DECEMBER 16
Dear Dee,

All my life I wanted a dog. I'd dream about us running together along the beach, tossing a Frisbee, or chasing a ball. I'd name him Gordy. I'd tell him my secrets and he'd tell me his. Gordy would be my very best friend.

Long ago Mom and Dad knew about my dog fever. They promised we'd get a golden retriever when Ezra was a little older. . . . So in the meantime, I collected ceramic replicas of every dog known to man. My shelves were lined with hunting dogs and poodles, terriers and sheepdogs, boxers and Chihuahuas. My room looked like a freaking animal shelter. Mom and Dad humored me with stuffed animals, goldfish, turtles, everything but a partridge in a pear tree. Now Christmas is only eleven days away and we're finally getting a dog. For EZRA. Not for me. A beautiful golden will come to live at 22 Elm and he will belong to my brother . . . not to me. This golden is a service dog trained to help special needs kids attach to animals rather than *things*. So I have to step aside and watch them "bond" for eight long weeks. A furry golden with big brown eyes will live in our house, play in our yard, and sleep in Ezra's room. But he's off limits for me. SO. NOT. FAIR.

Oh how I'd love to sneak into Ezra's room while he's asleep and play with Willy as long as I want. Oh how I'd love to shout out, "You can't keep me away . . . just you try . . . I have SPECIAL NEEDS too!!!" Let me count the ways.

DECEMBER 17
Dear Dee,

Countdown to Christmas: ten more days. Brought home our Christmas tree today which we all decorated. Even Ez stopped his videos to watch us string lights. The holiday excitement could have been "too muchness" for Ez, but it wasn't. He was fascinated with the blinking lights and joined in the Christmas spirit. I think Willy is the best therapy yet!! He really is making a difference.

Zoe and I are going to the school Christmas dance. Most kids are going alone or in groups. I'm giving up on Tyler but maybe someone else will drop from the sky? Tomorrow we're going to shop for *the* spectacular dress. Step aside Serena Spencer, here we come. Drum rolls please.

DECEMBER 18

Hey Dee,

Got an e-mail from Megan:

> *Thanks for being there, Jen, and letting me tell my story.
> I don't do this often and I feel radically better because of
> it . . . and you.*
>
> *Your grateful friend,*
>
> *Megan*

My reply:

> *I'm so glad you told me, Meg. I now think everyone has
> a story. Soon I will tell you mine.*
>
> *Always your friend,*
>
> *Jen*

DECEMBER 19

Hey Dee,

Zoe and I had a heart-to-heart. She told me I was probably the biggest reason she won the election for class president and thanked me a gazillion times. I reminded her that we were friends since before we were born so of course I would always be there for her whenever and wherever she wants me.

We never talked directly about Megan or Zoe being tight with Ashley. We didn't need to. She knows and I know . . . we'll be friends for life.

Now the four of us are going to the Christmas dance together.

DECEMBER 21

Dear Dee,

The Too Many said we could move forward with the project, but he wants to meet with us every week to discuss each section. "I want to meet with Mr. Alter regularly and approve of the material before it is in print." Said while hiking up his trousers and sniffing the air.

Wonder what it will take for HH to approve.

DECEMBER 22

Dear Dee,

We got to the dance a tad late and I was sort of freaked walking into a room full of guys in suits and girls in updos. But once we formed a line-dance that snaked around the gym, even the most uptight among us began to relax. Then everyone began dancing with or without a partner. Tony Ramirez danced a few with me. When Geoffrey Ellis and I did a fast dance, the crowd cleared the floor for our impromptu number. Aaron Green wanted to talk, talk, talk, but Sheldon Klaus just stood there and I had to talk, talk, talk.

Brad wasn't there. He was out of town on a political retreat. Not sure he would have come anyway. Too busy being Gonzo.

I had an OK time, sort of.

DECEMBER 23

Dear Dee,

I checked the store yesterday to see what Aviva was up to. She was working at her computer and Dad was with a customer. No implicating evidence. Feeling no widgets either.

DECEMBER 24
Dear Dee,

Nothing like last-minute shopping. But it seemed like everyone in Evanston was racing around like crazy mad chickens without their heads. Got Dad two golf shirts I know he'll love. For Mom, a bubble bath set. For Zoe, a bottle of floral perfume, and for Megan, a charm necklace with a pen charm, perfect for a fellow journalist!

And what to get for Ezra? A real friend is what I want, but they're not for sale at Macy's. I settled on a few DVDs and a leash for Willy who *has* become his special friend.

LATER
Hey Dee,

We gathered around the tree tonight, sang songs, and stuffed ourselves with Christmas cookies. Both Mom and Dad were really upbeat. Didn't want the night to end. Part of the thrill of Christmas is trying to guess what's inside the presents piled beneath the tree. I asked Ez what he thought was in each wrapping.

"A box," he said without a blink.

Can't argue with that.

DECEMBER 25
Dear Dee,

Christmas arrives.

I hit the jackpot. I got an awesome magenta cashmere sweater from Mom and Dad, an iPhone I've been wanting all year, and

The Girls in the Balcony, about the history of women journalists. Mom and Dad were so right on. They offered to send me to the Indiana program and said they would buy me a ticket in a heartbeat. Oh, how I would love to go. Sometimes I think I will. Ez now has Willy and often he doesn't even notice I'm there. Beginning to think my leaving problem is more about me than him.

Megan got the perfect gift for me: a beautiful leather diary with my initials engraved on the cover. The year is coming to an end and I am writing in your last pages, Dee. What an amazing choice. It's from Meg . . . so of course!!! But Ez's present was . . . well, Ez's gift I'll remember forever.

My brother got me a *Broadway Revisited* CD, reviewing the best of Broadway musicals including *My Fair Lady.* Mom said it was his idea.

"You think?" I asked.

"I know," she said.

OMG! Do you realize what that means, Dee? Ezra actually knew what I wanted even if he didn't want it himself! That means Ezra can *imagine.* He can put himself in someone else's shoes and *imagine* what they want! And they said it couldn't be done.

I began thinking . . . maybe . . . someday . . . Ezra might have a life with friends and a partner and a job, and enjoy things other than Nintendo and videos and ads for Excedrin PM.

Mom and I stared at each other in silence. I'm sure we were thinking the same thing. We didn't dare say it out loud. Other Christmas presents were on target, but nothing came close to Ezra's.

Gram and Gramps Wilson got me a hand-knit hat and scarf. Soft wool, wrong colors—black and pea green. I was gracious . . . I think. Granny and Grandpa Lauler got me a brown leather, shoulder-strap purse filled with cosmetics. I think it came right off Lauler's shelves, but whatever.

DECEMBER 26
Dear Dee,

No school, and a great day for forts and snowballs. The snow was wet and packable so everyone and his brother, literally, came to help build our fab snowman. We dressed him with mittens, belts, scarves, and a snazzy wooden pipe. We crowned him with a baseball cap, Cubs, of course. Ez gave him an old cell phone "so he can call for help when he begins to melt."

Now honestly, Dee, does that sound like someone with zero empathy and no imagination?

DECEMBER 27
Hey Dee,

Willy adores the snow. He has tons of fun running back and forth, back and forth, kicking up fresh flakes, racing between kids in a snowball fight. Even though he is Ez's dog, Willy follows me around. I try hard to keep my distance because Willy and Ez are a cool duo. I really don't want to interfere.

Reminds me of when I tried to make friends with some kids in Ezra's class and invite them over for Ez. But the whole thing backfired when they wanted to spend time with me instead of him. Sometimes I think I should step aside and let Ezra find his way on his own. Lately I've been trying to give him more space and most of the time it works! But I still worry. It only takes one lapsed moment for him to leap in front of a moving car.

DECEMBER 28
Dear Dee,

We're planning a New Year's Eve party with just us SCOOPers . . . nobody else allowed. Sure I want to look good and be noticed, but when I am with these kids, I don't have to dress in trendy clothes. The SCOOP crowd is where I belong, where I can be myself. While not every SCOOPer is my friend, they all care about something other than designer jeans and brand-name boots. None of us are mainstreamers . . . just a little off-beat. Maybe all of us think we're misfits, and maybe we are. But when we hang out, we fit together just fine.

DECEMBER 29
Dee,

I really did it this time. I ignited a firestorm.

I seriously messed up our DVD and froze all the bells and whistles on the TV. After hours of trying to fix it, I gave it to Ez, who's a whiz at most things tech. The kid came close to "unfreezing" the picture, which is amazing because it was beyond busted.

While Ez was working on the freaking thing, Dad came home and instantly assumed it was Ezra who screwed up the TV. He started in on him quietly at first, then got louder and louder.

"You interrupt our TV programs, you bust the DVD, you're rude to our family and friends, and it's high time you start to behave, young man. You can do better than this, Ezra. I know you can."

"I didn't bust the DVD," Ezra shouts. "I didn't freeze the DVD. You are wrong," he says. "I didn't hurt the DVD."

Mom stormed out of the kitchen and let Dad have it. She told him Ezra was not to blame for the broken DVD and that he was close to fixing the darn thing until his father started railing. Then the final blow: "What's more important, George, your precious high-tech toys or your only son?" Dad stomped out of the room, bolted out the door and took off . . . where?? I don't know!!

This whole thing started because of me. There's no getting around it. When anything in our house is broken, Dad automatically blames Ezra. Even when I'm the culprit. I hate that I can get away with everything when Ez gets away with nothing. Sometimes I'll cop to crimes I've never committed just to let him off the hook.

Like the time Dad shouted, "Who trekked mud in the house?"

"I did," I said, covering for Ez. "I did and I'm sorry."

"No, it's not true," Ezra fessed up. "I got mud on my shoes. I brought mud in our house. Jenny didn't bring mud in the house. I did."

Poor Ez can't say, "Not me, Dad, maybe my sister Jenny did, but not me, Dad." Ez has to speak the whole truth and nothing but the truth, even if it gets him in trouble. He just doesn't get the big picture. Just the facts, ma'am, just the facts.

This time I really am the one to blame. Dad blew up at Ez, Mom blew up at Dad, and Dad may never come home again. Well done, Jennifer Lauler, well done! How do you apologize for this one, Dee? Whoops, sorry folks, didn't really mean to destroy the family. I promise I'll never do it again.

DECEMBER 30

Dear Dee,

Couldn't sleep last night until I heard Dad's car in the garage and his key in the door. Thought it was parents who were supposed to stay up 'til their kids come home at night.

DECEMBER 31

Dear Dee,

Mom and Dad went to a New Year's Eve party together! Looks like they are friends again. Ezra is with Gram and Gramps Wilson so can you believe? We can all go out on the same night. Woo hoo!!

All of us SCOOPs piled into Samantha's basement and had a blast. Tony Ramirez played the guitar and Alvin Morgan tried to be cool with a solo dance. He was clumsy and tripped on his shoes but no one cared. We did impressions of Foxy and Mitchell and Fletcher, asking everyone to guess who. Brad did a hilarious impression of you-know-who. Chest forward, rigid strut, hairpiece askew, lips not moving. I loved it. When midnight came and the big ball dropped, kids paired off and I was left standing there alone. OMG what do I do? Then Brad came over and took my hand. Before I knew it I was in the middle of *the* most unforgettable kiss ever. Brad Neuworth is the genuine article.

Tyler, my friend, you can go to . . . Hartford, Hereford, and Hampshire, as Henry Higgins would say. Or go wherever, whenever, but ASAP.

JANUARY:
A NEU WORTH

JANUARY 1

Dear Dee,

A new year, and thanks to Meg, a beautiful new diary, with fresh, clean pages. Not bad for starters!

New Year's Resolutions

My list could fill another diary . . . but here are my top ten.

1. Don't blow it with Brad.

2. Keep Mom and Dad happy and together.

3. Don't blow it with Brad.

4. Be more cool with Ezra.

5. Exercise daily, 'til it hurts.

6. Cut down on sweets and junk food.

7. Jump-start writing the exposé.

8. Don't blow it with Brad.

9. Get over my problem with leaving Ez.

10. Control snarkiness with HH.

JANUARY 2
Dear Dee,

Started rehearsals again for *Fair Lady* and we're already sounding like pros. Think Mom and Dad will be in the audience. But together?? . . . Still not sure.

Didn't see Brad at SCOOP or in any of our classes. Did New Year's Eve spoil a really neat friendship?

JANUARY 3
Dear Dee,

Still no Brad sightings.

JANUARY 4
Dear Dee,

Finally heard about Brad at SCOOP. He has a high fever and swollen glands and feels HORRIBLE. The doctor said he has mono, should stay home, get plenty of rest, and drink lots of fluids. We all know the drill. MONO . . . the kissing disease! Whoops. If I get it, frankly, the price will be worth it.

JANUARY 5
Hey Dee,

Got an e-mail from Brad. He must have read my mind.

Hey J,

Where have you been? I've been held captive for almost a week, cut off from every human under forty and life as I knew it. They feed me bread and water and keep very close surveillance. Contact from the outer world, especially from the female persuasion, would put me in heaven. Can be reached by mobile phone, landline, text message, e-mail, or spiritual channeling. Negotiated ransom possible.

Cell number . . . so to speak . . . is: (312) 555-0004. Call any time, day or night, can't tell the difference anyhow.

Barely Bradley

My reply:

Hey Barely,

What a bummer, Brad. Really sorry to hear you are in jail and cannot pass "go" or collect $200. You never did say what your crime was. I will try to arrange for your release by negotiating a ransom. Would a batch of magazines help while you're in prison? Would my $10.25 in savings be enough to set you free? I will visit beneath your cell window some time tomorrow. Is that OK? Should I bring my piggy bank?

Please advise,

Jennifer Lauler, Director of Legal Aid

His reply:

Dear Director,

Yes, yes, yes, do come beneath my cell window and bring a ladder. Don't need magazines, just need JL. Let me know when you'll visit. I'll wear the coolest striped prison suit for the occasion.

Already counting,

Brad

JANUARY 7
Dear Dee,

Called Brad before I arrived. Wanted to make sure a visit was OK. "You've got to be kidding," he said. "I am suffering from terminal boredom which only you can cure. I'm already at the window. Did you find a ladder?"

JANUARY 9
Dear Dee,

When I got to his house, Brad was hanging out the window like a golden retriever. He looked so cute in his bathrobe with a big Bradley smile. We looked like *Romeo and Juliet* in reverse. Hope we have a different ending.

I updated him on the project and gave him all the news that isn't fit to print: Tyler and Serena broke up, again. Zoe is getting private intel for the project, the basketball team captain was suspended, and HH is still sniffing. "You're a great reporter," he said with a smile in his voice. "You ought to write for our school newspaper."

JANUARY 10
Dear Dee,

At dinner tonight, Mom and Dad were chatting away like always. Ez assaulted us with non-stop commercials: "Activia, Claritin,

Geico, Like a Good Neighbor. Go Like a Pro." His monologue ended with a hearty "VIVA VIAGRA," and began all over again. I've heard Ezra's commercial rants over half my life. This time it hit me as totally bizarre.

Mom and Dad never seem to mind. How do they do it year after year after year?

JANUARY 15
Hi Dee,

Today was our first SCOOP meeting since Brad's been back. I was shuffling papers when he was looking at me. He was shuffling papers when I looked at him. Our eyes met once and we couldn't hide the grin.

JANUARY 17
Dear Dee,

Last night Ez worked for hours on a series of story math problems assigned by Ms. Fletcher. He can do all kinds of math if they don't involve written paragraphs, and I have to admit, this one was a doozy. Mom and Dad patiently helped him figure out the problems and after many hours of careful coaching something clicked. Ez could solve even the hardest math and marched around the house like a proud soldier. What a kick. Like Henry Higgins we sang, "He's got it, we think he's got it." And he did!!

Then this morning Ez was all hopped up, eager to show Ms. Fletcher his math homework. When he got to class, he reached in his backpack and . . . the worksheet was gone. It had totally vanished, disappeared, was for sure not there. His teacher sends for me ASAP. I race upstairs two at a time to get to his classroom. I find Ezra completely melting down like I've never seen before. Ez is sitting, bent over with his head in his hands. His eyes are swollen, he's biting the inside of his cheek and I'm not sure he knows who I am.

I searched his backpack, his locker, and later, Mom scoured every inch of the house. The worksheet had mysteriously disappeared and we don't have a clue how. I won't rest until I know!

JANUARY 18
Hey Dee,

Zoe is now my "private eye" partner, gathering intel on worksheet suspects. Ms. Fletcher gave Ezra another chance and another worksheet. Ez reworked the math problems and he and I hand-carried the worksheet to Fletcher. "You did an absolutely remarkable job, Ezra," she rhapsodized. He almost looked relieved. Twice a day every day he asks, "Where is my first worksheet, Jenny?" The crisis may be over, but definitely not forgotten.

When we were little, Zoe and I used to play "I Spy." "I spy something green or blue or sharp or jagged." The other one would guess the object. Now we're real partners in a private investigation. And this is no game. No way. She texts me about possible worksheet suspects and gives intel on the creeps who loiter the halls. I now have a bully file and it's starting to bulge.

JANUARY 19
Hey Dee,

Tony Ramirez is Serena's newest flavor of the month. Wonder how long this will last?

JANUARY 20

Came home today and found Dad in his study and Mom in her room with the door shut. Unusual for Mom. "What's up?" I ask Ez.

"The ceiling," he said.

Whoops . . . forgot. It would be great if Ezra could be my private eye partner. If I spaz out about Mom and Dad, he could fill in the blanks, shed some light, or at least join me in the darkness.

JANUARY 21

Dear Dee,

Dad took Ez to the video store and Mom and I had a night out. What a treat. We went to the EAT Café and had dinner together.

I told her about Pit Bull being the chief suspect with the scissors. She made me promise to tell her if it happens again. "But don't tell Gramps," she said. "If he finds out, he'll promptly storm into City Hall, pound the table, and DEMAND attention be paid."

After scarfing down too much cake, I asked her about Ez when he was small. For my term paper, you understand. Felt I was prying, but Mom was ready to talk.

"Oh dear," she said, taking a deep breath. "Where do I start?

"In the delivery room, they handed me a beautiful baby boy with creamy skin and not a mark on his face. We had a wonderful stay in the hospital and came home to a cozy nursery waiting for his arrival. From the start, he had trouble nursing. He cried through the night and slept through the day. I was always worried and always exhausted."

Mom was telling this as though it happened yesterday.

"I called Dr. Felix so often I was sure he'd start blocking my calls. He said Ez had colic and it would take a few months before his digestive system got in gear. But digestion was hardly the worst of it. Ez shrieked with pain during the simplest of everyday routines. Putting him in the high chair, placing him in the stroller, bathing him, dressing him, you name it, it was sheer torture for him and for me. His screams were so piercing, I thought the neighbors would report me to child protective services.

"The hardest part was his not cuddling, not smiling back, not caring if I were there. He seemed unhappy with my very touch and avoided my gaze when I picked him up. It was so different with you, Jen. You were lively and bubbly the moment you opened your eyes. You squealed with joy when I walked in your room, and raised your arms to be picked up, to be held, to be loved."

I quickly changed the subject. "What was Ez like when he was two or three?" As if I didn't know.

"They promised me he'd come alive when he could walk and talk and engage the world on his own terms. But most of the time he'd stare at the ceiling and watch the fan go round and round. I was sure something was wrong. But Dad insisted Ez was just a different sort of kid who would develop on his own schedule. He kept reminding me that Ez was not only a boy but a second child and just didn't develop at the same rate as his sister."

"Did you believe him?" I asked.

"Oh, I so wanted to believe him, especially when our pediatrician was saying the same thing. Dr. Felix told us to wait 'til Ezra was four or five before we jumped to conclusions. I didn't need to wait and see. I already knew we had a serious problem.

"Finally we consulted a specialist who referred us to another and yet another who disagreed with the next and the one after that. Dad was fed up with the 'experts.' 'You go to a doctor with a problem,' he'd say, 'and if they're worth a damn, they'll tell you what's wrong and what to do about it. These yo-yos keep shaking their heads and handing us over to someone else.'

"Dad and I were usually on the same page with most things but not so with Ez. We finally agreed on a therapeutic program where Ezra made progress with language but still preferred toy cars to people . . . with the exception of you.

"Now fast forward. Dad has reversed his position. He claims I overprotect Ez and he would be better off in a residential program. I will not have it. I went through a lot of years blaming myself and I am now well over that mea culpa stage. I don't need your father or grandfather or grandmother telling me how to manage my son. I know what's best for Ezra and what's best is what he will have."

JANUARY 23
Hi Dee,

Been thinking about yesterday with Mom. Whenever they compare Ez and me, my mood sinks like a fallen soufflé. He was dealt a bad hand. I wasn't. He got the short end of the stick, I didn't. I know that. I will try with everything I have to make his life better. But please don't tell me I've been the "chosen one," the one good fortune smiled upon, the one who reminds them of what Ezra is not.

JANUARY 24
Dee,

Guess why I opt for campaign manager rather than class president like Zoe? Mom's on to me. She knows what this is about. Natch. She said that holding myself back for Ez helps neither him nor me. "Being class president, Jen, really won't make Ez feel like he's nothing better than the class clown. He'll advance at his pace and you'll advance at yours. Go for it, Jen," she cheered. "You know, we're right behind you."

I think I'm slowly beginning to "get it."

JANUARY 25
Hi Dee,

Mom and Dad asked about the Indiana writers' program. I told them I plan to apply and this time I think I really mean it.

JANUARY 26
Dear Dee,

I found an application on my desktop this morning.

They're not so good at "subtle" but oh so good to me!

JANUARY 27
Dear Dee,

Brad asked if I'd like to go to the movies with him this weekend. OMG. *Bradley Neuworth, why has it taken you so long?*

JANUARY 28
Dear Dee,

I said "yes" to the movies . . . now Mom has to say "yes" to me.

JANUARY 29
Dear Dee,

Mom said OK. Dad wants to know who else is going and wants me home no later than 10:00.

Strange . . . I'm old enough to take care of Ezra, but not old enough to be out past 10:00 pm.

JANUARY 30
Hey Dee,

Can't concentrate on math or the Civil War. Having a crush is a severe form of mental illness. They'll never find a cure!

JANUARY 31
Hey Dee,

We saw *Juno* and I was so excited to be out with Brad, I may have laughed in all the wrong places. After the movie, we went to the EAT Café and a ton of Roosevelt kids were there. I loved having half the school see Brad and me together, not just as SCOOPers either. Eat your heart out at the EAT Café, Tyler what's-your-name.

We talked about SCOOP and HH, about tennis and hockey and Serena and *My Fair Lady*. We talked and talked and lost track of time. Sometimes I think I've known Brad forever and sometimes it feels like he suddenly parachuted into my life and nothing will ever be the same.

FEBRUARY:
TO BE OR NOT TO
BE ... MY VALENTINE

FEBRUARY 1

Dear Dee,

All of us SCOOPs are planning a ski trip to Boyne Mountain. Guess Dad will want to chaperone.

FEBRUARY 2

I told Ez I was thinking about going to Boyne Mountain for a ski weekend with my friends. "Can I come, Jenny? Can I go to Boyne Mountain with Willy?" he shouts like I live in Australia. Ezra is not as graceless as some, but he has trouble balancing on skates and cross-country skis. I promised I'd take him skiing to prepare him for a trip sometime soon.

"When is soon? When is soon, Jenny?" he asked, pulling at his ear.

"In a few weeks," I said.

"How many is a few? A few is how many?"

I said three, grabbing a number out of thin air. Sometimes I try to help him stretch his mind to focus on something he can't measure in numbers. I try but . . .

FEBRUARY 3

Hi Dee,

I remember when Ez was little and couldn't look you in the eye. Every week his therapist would come to the house to teach him to make eye contact when someone's talking to him. She'd place two chairs opposite one another and sit face-to-face with Ezra. She would cup her hands around his cheeks and help him cast his eyes in her direction. When he gradually forced himself to meet her eyes, she'd hand him a crummy old chocolate chip cookie. Then, twice weekly, Mom would drive him to therapy where he'd struggle through the same routine. We'd sit in the waiting room while Ezra cried from the therapy room. Mom stared at a magazine, eyes never moving. I'd hide inside my hair and watch my watch.

I always wondered if my brother was shrieking from pain, fear, or stored-up rage. We never knew. If he knew, he couldn't say. That's been the worst of it for me. Even now I'd like to put my hand on his shoulder—if he could stand it—and say, "Just tell me what's wrong, Ez. What's upsetting you? Just tell me about it and maybe I can make it better."

I can see those scenes like videos in my head. Moms and dads would sit beside their kid with autism, often with a brother or sister. The ones brought for therapy hid behind books they never read. Others would thread a string between their fingers again and again and again. Most just stared at the overhead lights. You could tell which kids were there to get help, and which were along for the ride. I wondered if they wondered which one I was.

FEBRUARY 4

Dear Dee,

All the SCOOPers are going to Boyne Mountain. Mr. Stone, our P. E. teacher, will be the chaperone. Sorry, Dad.

FEBRUARY 6

Dear Dee,

Guess what? Brad's coming with us to Boyne Mountain.

Watch me fall on my face.

FEBRUARY 7

Hey Dee,

The weekend was a blast. I wasn't the best skier on the slopes but I didn't fall on my face either. Brad and I got to hang out a lot. Wow! If grown-ups care more for each other than this . . . I'm not sure I'll make it.

FEBRUARY 8

Dee,

Serena Spencer is giving Brad the eye. He doesn't give her the time of day. Whoo hoo!!

FEBRUARY 9

Hi Dee,

Writing my term paper for Ms. Mitchell, I flashed back to when Ez was almost five and I was almost eight. He could speak clearly by then, but had huge problems with pronouns. He'd reverse them, ignore them, turn them inside-out. Mom and I practiced with him until he got it right. Each time he made a mistake, Mom would deny him a cookie. When he got it right, he'd get the cookie. If he could speak proper English, Mom thought maybe then he'd connect with people rather than water fountains and moving trains.

Our first task was to end his "echoing" craze.

"Do you want a cookie?" Mom would ask.

"You want a cookie," he'd repeat.

Then Mom would say "I want a cookie" and she'd get a cookie after saying "I."

We'd repeat the drill until Ez could say the expected "I." Then he'd get his cookie. After endless drills and cookies, Ezra got it right. WE felt the struggle was worth it. Not sure he felt the same.

Mom and I began a shared mission. She would teach Ezra to read other people's body language and name the feelings it expressed. She would teach him to hold a TWO-WAY conversation. That was the grand plan, Dee, and we were determined to make it work.

FEBRUARY 10
Dear Dee,

Remember the grand plan?

So, Mom sat in on Ez's therapy sessions and learned to do their "interaction drills." We later practiced at home. After school, we'd set up a lab with flash cards of smiley faces, frowning faces, kids looking sad or mad or big-eyed and scared. Then we'd teach Ez to name each feeling. After he labeled the feeling correctly, we'd describe a scene that prompted that feeling. "If David's little sister tore up his drawing, what would David feel?" Or "If she

spilled paint on your brand new shirt, what would you feel?"
"Wet," he said.

Ez made real progress during his exercises. But spontaneous chit-chat was another story. Not long ago Caleb O'Riley ran through our neighborhood telling us his dog had squeezed under the fence bordering their yard. Caleb was terrified when his dog was lost. Mom asked if his dog had been found. Ezra asked for the measurements of the fence.

Ez is now in a social support group where he's taught to make "small talk." He's learning how to begin a conversation, what to ask, and how to listen. After a long, hard working session he asked, "What's so great about small talk? I do large talk. A debate over Adidas vs. Reeboks does not at all interest me."

The boy has a point.

FEBRUARY 11

Recently I realized that Ezra is not only blind to other people's emotions, he is totally clueless about his own. Mom always said he was absolutely fearless when crossing a busy intersection or running across a footbridge. I remember with horror a day not so long ago.

We were walking alongside a bike path, Ezra on the road. Along came a speeding car, and Ezra would not move out of its way. I tried pulling him to safety but he insisted on his "right of way." That's when I learned that Ez does not have a built-in alarm system. He is perfectly capable of darting into traffic or diving into a waterless pool. He doesn't really recognize disaster. No wonder I need that invisible cord.

FEBRUARY 12

Dear Dee,

I found out that Mom and Dad now agree that Ez doesn't need a sleep-away school. I think he's doing better mostly because of Willy. That's my opinion and I'm Dr. Jennifer Lee Lauler!

FEBRUARY 13

Dear Dee,

Was at Lauler's Luggage today. Aviva hasn't stopped smiling or batting her eyes at Dad. But Dad was more taken with the new shipment of brown leather cases. Like father, like son.

FEBRUARY 14

Hi Dee,

Dad's planning to take Mom out for Valentine's Day. He asked if I'd watch Ez. Are you kidding? Heck yes!

LATER

I'm getting a Valentine's Day card for Brad. But I won't give it unless he gives me one first.

LATER

Decided to give him one anyway.

LATER

Decided not to. If I give him one first, he'll give me one only because I gave him one.

LATER

Gave him one anyway. Didn't get one from him.

FEBRUARY 15

Got one from Brad . . . too late and too bland. But hey, got a card from Brad.

FEBRUARY 16

Dear Dee,

A very sweet guy in 10th grade came to my locker today.

"I found this paper with your brother's name on it," he said shyly. "I thought you might want to see it."

"Where did you find it?" I shrieked, not even thanking the poor kid.

"I found it crumpled up in the library book I was reading," he mumbled.

"D-d-d-d-do you r-r-remember which book?" I stammered.

"What's the big deal?" he asked.

"I need to know," I said urgently.

"*To Kill a Mockingbird,*" he said, shrugging his shoulders.

I shot over to the library, found *Mockingbird,* and looked at the names of people who had signed it out. There it was, in bold black letters. Francine Bayler, aka Pit Bull, January 17, when the worksheet went missing. Can you believe it? That snake stole the worksheet Ez worked so hard to complete. She crushed his spirit as she had his sheet.

She can pin him against the wall, lock him in place with her klutzy boots and he'll survive. But this brand of viciousness is outrageous. Who gets their jollies from scaring innocent kids? I can't wrap my mind around that frickin' monster. I thought I had frightened her into civility. But maybe that's impossible. First she pinned him against the wall, then the scissors, I think, and now the math worksheet. How do I stop this craziness??? How?

FEBRUARY 17

Dear Dee,

Francine is stronger, broader, and taller than my brother. But Ezra is a giant compared to her. He always will be.

FEBRUARY 18

Hi Dee,

I feel like telling Gramps about Pit Bull, after all. Together we'd storm City Hall and attention WOULD be paid.

FEBRUARY 19

Dear Dee,

Mr. Alter and I finally told The Too Many what we're planning to include in our exposé. We put our cards on the table and said we will gather as much information as possible about school bullies who target and terrify kids on school yards and lunchrooms or places rarely monitored.

HH was quiet for a time. Then he began sniffing, sniffing as though he smelled a rotten egg. He nervously hiked up his trousers and avoided my glance. I waited 'til forever before he snorted a response. "Well, Jennifer," he said, a bad sign. "We have to be careful with allegations that may not be easy to prove. I certainly do appreciate what you are doing at SCOOP, but I need some time to consider all possible consequences before you make specific accusations, if you will."

Though my heart was thumping like a bongo drum, I said, "But Mr. Harrington, we really have to consider the consequences of NOT doing anything, of NOT reporting what is happening."

I don't know where I got the nerve; the words just popped out like a jack-in-the-box. Then again, I would have felt rotten if I caved in. With head tilted, jaw thrust forward, and nostrils flaring, HH said he was well aware of the problem and everyone at Roosevelt is working on it. Really? WORKING ON IT?

FEBRUARY 22
Dear Dee,

Today's rehearsal for *Fair Lady* was awesome. Though Tyler, The Magnificent, can only sing one note, the chorus sounds like pros, the costumes will be gorgeous, and the sets for the Embassy Ball are breathtaking. I think we're almost as good as an honest-to-goodness Broadway production. Brad promised to come the first night with his buddies. Don't know yet about Mom and Dad.

FEBRUARY 23
Hey Dee,

In study hall today I was writing Brad's name in my notebook. When I wrote Neuworth in various styles of calligraphy, I realized there is a message in his name. Brad is literally a "new worth" in my life. Granny Lauler told me that the magic of first love is our ignorance that it will ever end. Not so for yours truly. Always braced for a so long, farewell, see ya, goodbye. I know, I'm certifiable. It runs in the family.

FEBRUARY 24
Dee,

Do you think Brad writes my name in his notebook, like I do his? So, Henry Higgins, why can't he be like me?

FEBRUARY 25

Dear Dee,

I googled Aviva last night and discovered she is 39, was in regional theater, and is divorced. Not exactly what I was hoping for.

FEBRUARY 26

Dear Dee,

When I used to nervously tap my foot on the floor or rake my fingers through my hair, I'd think I was a milder version of Ezra. Sometimes I think my clinging to people is a way of being . . . not Ezra. He frantically runs away, I frantically run toward. Opposite sides of the same coin. I'd love to talk to Brad about it, *if* I could talk to Brad about it.

FEBRUARY 27

Hey Dee,

Midterms are next week. My brain hurts.

FEBRUARY 28

Dear Dee,

Ezra and Willy are a match made in heaven! Every morning Ez rises with the sun to fill Willy's dish with fresh water and food. He brushes his coat, strokes him gently, and showers him with toys. Their bedtime ritual is a scene from a picture book. Ez drapes his arm around Willy and falls asleep with a blissful smile.

Last week we discovered a lump on Willy's thigh. We took him to Dr. Burrow who said the thing definitely had to come out. Though Ezra was really freaked about Willy's health, he did everything possible to make him well. He got up in the middle of the night and gave him meds—not an easy task—refilled his water dish, and tenderly smoothed his fur. It blew my mind. Ez treats Willy the way we treat Ez. Somewhere inside Ez knows about love. He has it for Willy, and maybe for us?

I figured out why Ez is attached to Willy. When they look each other in the eye, neither asks anything more. They read each other's signals without speaking a word. Willy doesn't force Ez to talk, to sit up straight, to quit looking at the sky. And he enjoys Ez's riffs. He perks his ears when he hears Geico, Viagra, and AT&T. When Ez walks him around the block, people ask about his beautiful dog. He proudly tells them about Willy's breed. He has an easier time talking to strangers while patting his dog. Willy has become a bridge between Ezra and the world. I honestly think he's replaced me. Willy is now my brother's keeper.

FEBRUARY 29
Hi Dee,

There is a sweet kid in Ezra's special ed class who shares his love of dogs and video games. Recently Ez and Jonathan began calling each other comparing notes on games. Though Willy is Ez's very best friend, Jonathan is an almost-buddy who walks on two feet and doesn't bark. Oh sure, it's not like Zoe and Meg and me, but at least my brother has something like a friend. That's a big deal, Dee. I can't celebrate yet. Too worried I'll jinx it.

MARCH: EYE SPY

MARCH 1
Dear Dee,

Told Mom and Dad it was Francine who stole the worksheet. They immediately reported her to HH who said he would speak to her and her parents that very evening. Yeah, and then what??

MARCH 2
Hey Dee,

Francine was not in school today. Suspension? Maybe, Please????

MARCH 4
Hi Dee,

Ezra's birthday is tomorrow and we've invited both sets of Grands and his friend Jonathan to his party. I decided to invite Brad even though it might be a deal breaker. But I want him to see our family up close and personal in all its exquisite glory.

MARCH 5
Hi Dee,

Gram and Gramps Wilson arrived with gifts and smiles and were completely wired for celebration. Ezra verges on comfortable around Gram and Gramps. He greeted them with a "how are you" without prompting. And it didn't feel rehearsed.

When Jonathan arrived, Ezra headed for the stairs to play his video games. We gently urged him to wait 'til his guests arrived and after the cake and ice cream. This made absolutely no sense to Ez. He obliged anyway. Jonathan started toward the videos and Ezra explained the ridiculous custom of waiting for guests to arrive.

Granny and Grandpa Lauler were the next to come. Grandpa has had a bad back and can no longer help out at Lauler's even during a busy season. He greeted Ezra with a big bear hug that made him lurch from its sheer weight and exuberance. Granny surveyed Ez for signs of maturity and was pleased when he thanked her for coming. Dad and Grandpa Lauler launched into their hockey talk, comparing notes about the Blackhawks and whether they have a chance at the Stanley Cup. So far, so good.

Then Brad made his entrance and Mom welcomed him with her easy charm. Brad was instantly relaxed, I could tell. I introduced "my friend" to the family and mentioned Brad's older brother played hockey in high school. Grandpa Lauler grabbed the opportunity to tell about his heroic football career when he was young: the touchdown pass that broke the tie, the sixty-yard run that scored the winning TD. Stories we've heard many times over, stories more grand with each telling. Brad smiled patiently. I hoped he, too, has a grandfather.

In a booming voice that made Willy quiver, Ezra protested that it wasn't a sixty-yard run that Grandpa made. "The last time you told the story it was forty yards, Grandpa."

"But who's counting?" Mom said, trying to clear the air.

"I beg your pardon, young man," Grandpa objected. "It was indeed a sixty-yard run and I have the newspaper clippings to prove it." He then told more elaborate stories of his service in the Korean War and his near-death experience as a naval pilot, all of which led to his lecture on the upcoming election.

"One of the candidates is from Illinois," Ezra bellowed. "And we want him to win the primaries and then live in the White House in Washington, DC, the District of Columbia."

Brad walked over to Ezra, patted his shoulder, and gave him a vigorous two thumbs up. Somehow Ez understood the gesture, and smiled from the top of his head to the tip of his toes.

OMG. I want to marry the guy.

I don't remember the ice cream and cake or anything that happened after that moment. When I walked Brad to the door, I said, "Well there you have it. This is the Lauler family. Now tell me what you think. An unedited version, please?"

"No offense, Jen, but I'd rather be stranded on a desert island with Ezra than with Grandpa Lauler any day." I fell into his arms and couldn't stop laughing.

Happy birthday, my dear brother. I hope this day was as special for you as it has been for me.

MARCH 6
Dear Dee,

Saw Aviva crossing the street in front of Lauler's. As she ran to make the green light, her purple scarf blew in the wind, she moved like a dancer, and heads turned from every direction. Drat!

MARCH 7

Dear Dee,

After school, Megan came home with me to work on the project. Ez greeted her at the door with, "You are very, very skinny."

"That's true," she said, letting the clumsy comment roll off her back.

We put our print-outs on my desk and were ready to go to work. Suddenly I saw my room through Megan's searching eyes. There was the lock on the door to keep Ez from prowling. Two badly repaired walls featured dents from Ezra's fists. My dog collection looked like Dr. Burrows' animal hospital. A collie with two and a half legs. A poodle without a head. A beagle with a broken tail. There were paint stains on the carpet and magic markers on the blinds.

Megan didn't have to ask what led me to the project. But she did, diplomatically. "You now know my story, Jen," she said softly. "So what drew *you* to the exposé?" I told her to look around my room. The story is literally written on the walls.

"Is it about your brother?" she asked gently.

I talked more openly than I ever had before. I told her about autism, and how it disconnects Ezra from people. I told her about how hard Ez tries to fit into a world he's not neatly wired for. I told her about the Pit Bulls at school and how I'm determined to stop them in their tracks. "There's so much I want to fix in this crazy world," I said throwing up my hands. "I don't even know where to begin. I wish I had known your father."

"I was thinking the same thing," she said.

MARCH 8

Hey Dee,

Meg and I are two of a kind. We both loved *The Kite Runner*, we both worry about "tomorrow" and we could call each other at 2 o'clock in the morning without having to say we're sorry.

MARCH 9

Hi Dee,

Rehearsal today was fantastic. I'm always on a high after singing in the chorus. I'm not exactly a Broadway star, but I have a great time pretending.

MARCH 10

Hi Dee,

Had lunch today with Zoe and her sister, Lucy. I used to spend tons of time at their house where I could be Ezra-free during a grand meltdown. Today was different.

Zoe was telling us about an executive meeting at school and the clash over the lunch menu: organic vs. regular. As she was getting fired up telling her story, she spilled mustard all over Lucy's beautiful new silk blouse, which she got for her sixteenth birthday. "Honestly, Zoe!" she shrieked. "Can you think about anything besides your STUPID class presidency? Could you consider for a minute what you are doing and saying and splattering all over innocent people?"

"And what about you, Ms. Extreme Princess?" Zoe sputtered. "Where do you get off wearing a silk blouse to a Weinerschnitzel lunch anyway?"

They bickered back and forth, digging up old hurts and blasting each other through a mustard-splattered lunch. They weren't about to call a truce anytime soon, so I decided to leave. When I did, they were still dueling like an average pair of teenage sisters. Neither of them noticed I was leaving, neither heard me say goodbye.

MARCH 11

Dee,

Weird what I felt watching Zoe and Lucy fight. I was secretly jealous of their shout-a-thon, each giving as good as she got. I didn't envy Lucy's mustard-stained blouse, but I did envy Zoe's license to let her anger rip, to openly hate her sister, if only for a day. That could never happen with Ez and me. I have to walk on eggshells, hoping to avoid a new dent in the wall or the next spontaneous combustion.

MARCH 12

Hi Dee,

Dad is going out of town for a whole week and Mom isn't going with him. That's a new one. Gram and Gramps Wilson always stayed with us when Mom and Dad travelled. Trips were few but when they happened, Dad never went without Mom. If she couldn't go, he wouldn't go.

What's happening, Dee?

MARCH 13

Hey Dee,

I heard them talking late into the night.

Another argument? Or not? Voices were too low. Couldn't tell.

MARCH 15
Dear Dee,

Mom was on the phone with Gram Wilson this afternoon. Just as I entered the room, she hung up like she was holding burning coal.

MARCH 16
Dear Dee,

I told Meg about envying Zoe when she fought with her sister. "That's really wacked, isn't it, Meg?"

"Oh, I can relate," she said. "If you're wacked, then I am too. I envy kids who can argue with their mothers. My mom now has to be two parents to two kids. . . . She doesn't really need any flack from me."

It must be true. Everyone and her sister has a story to tell.

MARCH 17
Hi Dee,

Working on my term paper last night, I remembered my "it isn't fair" outburst when I was about ten. Mom came home from an Autism Speaks meeting, and the first thing she said was, "Where's Ezra?"

"Hey, Mom, can you at least say hello before you ask for Ezra?" I squealed. "Ezra, Ezra, always Ezra. We go to doctors for Ezra, we practice drills for Ezra, we stay at home for Ezra, and we can't even have a dog because of—you guessed it—EZRA!!!!"

I hollered about Ezra getting into my room, going through my drawers, killing my goldfish, and wrecking my dog collection. Everything's about him. "Ezra, Ezra, always Ezra!!!"

Mom stopped and listened to every word. Looking at her fingertips, she said, "No, Jen, it isn't fair. It isn't fair to you, it isn't fair to Dad, and most of all it isn't fair to Ezra. I know he sucks up most of the energy in this family and I'm not surprised you feel edged out or pushed aside. You have every right to be angry, Jenny. I'm really, really sorry you feel like you've gotten a raw deal. And I want you to tell me every time you feel invisible, or worse yet, seen but thoroughly ignored."

I felt better after that outburst. And relieved, big time, that Mom didn't get mad. Actually, I had more to say but I didn't want to make things worse. When she listed the people "it isn't fair to," guess who was missing?

MARCH 18
Hi Dee,

Reliving my "it isn't fair" phase, some blurry memories came into focus. I remembered the time I ran home from school to show off a super report card to Mom and Dad. They said they were really proud. But Ezra was having a meltdown. They ran to the rescue, and I was left holding my As.

Since then I've gradually learned to be more like Gramps. Now I let them know ATTENTION MUST BE PAID. And it works, most of the time.

MARCH 19
Dear Dee,

Asked HH again if he's thought about what we planned for the SCOOP project. Speaking through his locked jaw, he said after his last meeting with Mr. Alter, he is very close to a decision. He said he will get back to us when he has the final answer. Translation: don't call us, we'll call you. If you will.

MARCH 20
Dear Dee,

Caught Pit Bill trying to bust into Ezra's locker. Ha! I sneak up behind her. "I've caught you red-handed," I shout loud enough for a crowd to gather. "And this time I have witnesses to prove you're the one."

She doesn't know what to expect next. Neither do I.

MARCH 21
Dear Dee,

Told Brad that The Too Many is stalling. We decided to go ahead with the writing but won't print without his approval. If he delays indefinitely, we will threaten to go to the superintendent of schools in Evanston. Now we just might have another headline: *Harris Harrington III obstructs report on abuse of special needs students. Get the real SCOOP here.*

MARCH 22
Hey Dee,

From time to time, most of us become wedded to a favorite word.

Mom likes *quintessential.*

Dad likes *bombastic.*

I like *astonishing.*

Ezra likes *road kill.*

Eighty-year-old Mrs. Canilloni brings us apples from her yard.

"Thank you, Mrs. Canilloni, that's very kind of you," I say.

"Your hair looks like road kill," Ezra offers.

And there are variations:

"You used to be a squirrel," he tells the mail carrier. "Now you're nothing but road kill."

Who says the boy has no imagination?

MARCH 23
Dear Dee,

Dad is away for a week. Mom is here, but her head is somewhere else.

I'm afraid to ask what's going on between them. Afraid to find out what I'm afraid I'll find out.

MARCH 24
Dee,

If they are going to divorce, how in the world would I explain it to Ez? "You see, Ez, Mom and Dad have been arguing and they've stopped being friends. And so Dad's going to move to a different house. And he's not going to live with us anymore. You and Willy and Mom and I will have to leave this house, the only one you've ever known, and we'll have to move to a smaller house where your whole world will be turned upside-down. Oh yes, I forgot to tell you, Ez, most of this is because of you."

MARCH 25
Dear Dee,

Dad's back but not really. At dinner he asked each of us about our day. In a big blustering voice, all noise, no inflection, Ez answers with a chorus of commercials.

I was next to talk. I told Dad about HH dragging his heels on the project and our running out of time. "What do you think we should do, Dad?" He looked at me vacantly and I realized he was totally checked out. "Earth to Dad, Earth to Dad," I say. I ask again. He's staring into space, rubbing the scar above his brow.

"Jenny is asking you a question, Dad. Jenny is asking you a question. You are not answering Jenny's question," Ezra persisted.

Way to go, Ez. Sometimes you're the only one who gets it.

MARCH 26
Dear Dee,

I found an old essay I once wrote called "Being Ezra."

I put myself in Ez's sneakers and wondered what it was like to be my brother. I imagined he had been plucked out of his natural habitat and dropped into a world that was too much for him. A world of too much noise and color and flashing lights. A world that speaks gibberish and insists he gibber, too. A world where he must talk to strangers and look them in the eye. If he turns around to look at the wall, they clamp his head in a human vise and make his eyes meet theirs. When he forces an eye in their direction, they then loosen their grip. Would he be happier playing with a string and staring at the sky?

MARCH 30

Hey Dee,

After school I met Brad at the EAT Café where we . . . ATE. My intel on Mom and Dad hasn't been encouraging, so I was quiet for longer than I knew. Brad wondered if it was about Ezra. "What's it been like for you with Ez?" he asked without a flicker of fake concern.

"Thanks for asking," I said. "No one ever has."

Stuff burst out of me like Mt. Vesuvius erupting. I told him about Ezra wandering away when he was little and I was in charge. I told him about wanting to squeeze the autism out of my brother and turn him into a regular boy. I told him about strangers stopping us on the street offering a catalog of kooky advice. Seriously, people come up with in-your-face testimonials about what we should do for Ezra. They tell us to give him mega vitamins or secretin or gluten-free food. Some railed against vaccines. "You know, dear, immunization shots cause autism, don't you, dear?" Everyone and their aunt Catherine had a miracle cure. I knew most of this stuff was garbage, but I wanted so much to believe we could find the magic elixir that would make my brother a happy kid.

After spilling out my guts, I felt lighter than a floating balloon. But what did Brad think of my emotional tsunami? After a long, quiet pause, he said something I'll never forget. "I always knew you were really cool, Jen, for the way you treat your brother and because you really know how to care." I think I will replay that message in my head over and over 'til the end of time.

MARCH 31

Dear Dee,

I asked Brad what his first three wishes were this very minute. He thought for a while. "I'll tell you, if you tell me," he said. I promised.

His first was to ace all his classes so he could choose the school he wants after he graduates. Second was to make the varsity tennis team in high school and third was to someday travel the world. Couldn't help noticing there was a big, fat zero, zilch about love or marriage. Or me.

I didn't feel like telling him mine. Too many about him.

APRIL:
INVISIBLE DIS-CORD

APRIL 1
Dear Dee,

Brad texted me last night and said, "hey JL, you never told yours."

APRIL 2
Dear Dee,

OK, not all my wishes are about Brad. But it would be amazing if we could be together for the next four years (or more?).

Top of my wish list is Ez. I wish that someday, he will make his way on his own, have a real friend, and a decent job. When I'm most extravagant, I wish he'll have a partner, whether or not they marry. If he can't make it alone, I'll take care of him when Mom and Dad no longer can. I can handle it. Not sure about Brad, though . . .

And I wish I could become the best journalist I can possibly be. I want to uncover serious injustices in the world. I want to be a voice for those who've lost their own. Yes, that's what I want to do after college. I want to make people with power listen to those who have none. When I heard about those Medill student journalists who proved some of the death row prisoners were innocent, I was blown away. Because of their work, our state actually repealed the death penalty. I hope someday I can do something of that magnitude. Something that makes a difference.

Some of these grand wishes I can tell Brad. Others? No.

APRIL 3
Dear Dee,

The Too Many called me into his office today. It got a little hairy. With pursed lips and a flushed face, he said, "It has come to my attention that your project is boldly implying that the Roosevelt faculty is not responding to the needs of targeted students. And that is totally unacceptable."

With my voice trembling, I stiffened my spine and said, "With all due respect, Mr. Harrington, the parents of targeted students claim when they report bullying behavior to faculty, teachers listen but take no action. Whether we print these complaints or not, families are talking and their anger is mounting."

HH raised his eyebrows and said, "Young lady, I will decide what is credible, what is anecdotal, what can be printed, and what should be thrown out as hearsay." He hiked up his trousers, snorted noisily and said, "I think our meeting has come to an end, Jennifer Lauler."

Wow, that is the best news of the day.

APRIL 4
Dear Dee,

After consulting with Mr. Alter, I talked to Mom and Dad about what our next move should be. Both said the project was too important to offend HH and put the thing in jeopardy. "The fight is not worth the risk," they said in unison. My fair-minded mom suggested we print what we have, concede the information about teachers is only anecdotal and make very clear that confirmation is pending. The woman is a genius.

APRIL 5
Hi Dee,

I overheard Mom talking to Gram Wilson about seeing a lawyer. Now I really have the widgets. My worries were NOT all in my head. I've got the widgets but not the guts to ask what's going on between them.

APRIL 6
Dear Dee,

Lately, I've noticed Ezra doesn't tie his shoes or comb his hair, doesn't brush his teeth or wear fresh clothing. Don't know if we're in for another long, stormy siege. Can't tell if he's going through his own variety of teenage hell or if he feels something's different between Mom and Dad. Or none of the above.

Dad hasn't taken another trip without Mom and he's home for dinner every night. That's the good news. But he still looks as lost in his world as Ezra does in his. He is pleasant, asks questions, and is more patient with Ez. Yet he moves slowly and looks at us with glazed eyes. It's like Willy after his surgery. He limps along, but barely.

APRIL 7
Dee,

Went to Lauler's today. Aviva's still showcasing her seriously white teeth and batting her seriously long lashes. She was in my father's office. They were looking at a spreadsheet, shoulders touching. The door was open so I walked in.

Dad usually lights up when I drop by. Today he looked fidgety, not quite inviting me to leave, but not asking me to stay either.

APRIL 8
Hey Dee,

Had a Eureka moment today!

I've been spending most of my time with Meg, my soul mate, Zoe, my ring-mate, and Brad, my future mate (ha ha) and SCOOP and the project and *My Fair Lady*. And guess what? Ez has been fine! Why did it take me so long to figure it out? I think I've been caught up in the spell of *that* day in the garden. And not even knowing it. It's like Ez is still four and I'm still seven, like he's about to get lost and I'm about to get blamed. Get real, Jennifer Lauler, *that* day was then and *this* one is now. Ez is twelve years old, and he has Willy and Jonathan, and of course Mom and Dad and a cell phone and words and enough smarts to get from here to there. Of course I'll always protect my brother, care for him, and try to keep him safe. But does caring for him mean I can't care for me? Enough of this "leaving" problem. I'm applying to the Indiana program tonight.

APRIL 9
Dear Dee,

I've decided. If the best school of journalism is away from home, that's where I'll go. I can come home for holidays and Ez can visit me at school. *Going* away isn't the same as *staying* away forever.

APRIL 10
Dear Dee,

I'm really going to miss *Fair Lady* at the final curtain. I'll miss the music and the songs and all the goofy times we've had at rehearsals. Hope we can find each other in another play in high school next year. Yikes—did I say high school? Next year? Really?

APRIL 11
Hi Dee,

Checked out Lauler's again. Aviva was leaving for lunch on the arm of a gorgeous hunk of a man. They say she's gaga over him.

Hope he's gaga over her.

APRIL 12
Dee,

Getting up the nerve to ask Mom.

I think.

APRIL 13
Hi Dee,

Mom came home from Autism Speaks chattering away about a new fundraiser she is organizing. "It's been so complicated," she said. "I even had to consult a lawyer."

Woo hoo! I cheered, not able to hide this huge jolt of joy. Things between them look promising, but why was Dad gone without Mom for an entire week?

APRIL 14
Dee,

OK, so the lawyer was for the fundraiser and not for a divorce. And Aviva has snagged someone other than my father. But for how long? And I still don't know where Dad went and with whom and why!

APRIL 15
Hi Dee,

But wait, why has Dad been soooo spacey, not talking to Mom and always staring at the chandelier?

APRIL 16
And what were they arguing about in hushed tones at night?

APRIL 17
Before I get up the nerve to talk to Mom, I told Zoe about Mom and Dad. "Count your blessings," she said. "My dad's never home long enough for them to fight."

Wow. That gave me something to think about.

APRIL 18
I'm going to ask tomorrow.

APRIL 19
So here's the deal.

Mom said Dad's been preoccupied lately because he's worried about the future of Lauler's Luggage. When he went to the convention in South Carolina, he had to admit that small independent stores like ours can no longer compete with the larger chains. He's been trying to decide what to do.

OK, so Dad was at a merchandise convention and came back with a ton of worries about Lauler's. But why were Mom and Dad arguing and what was it about?

Mom reminded me that spats take place between the best of friends. "Like you and Zoe," she said. "A few bumpy patches don't mean the end of the road. In fact, when the dust settles and your vision is clear, often things are even better than they were before."

So this is the story. Dad was away for a convention, he and Aviva were reviewing inventory shoulder-to-shoulder, Mom and Dad were having an ordinary spat and my imagination galloped faster than a Triple Crown winner. Maybe I should write fiction.

Moral of this story: when in doubt, ASK. Even if you're trembling in your knee-high boots . . . ASK.

MAY: AND THE WINNER IS

MAY 10

Dee,

Term paper is DONE! Woo! Now I just need to finish the bullying project and get through the last week of rehearsals for *My Fair Lady*. One down, two to go . . .

MAY 13

Dear Dee,

Ms. Mitchell wanted to see me after class today. OMG, was my term paper a bust?

She said she thought my paper on Ezra was extraordinary. Get that, she said "extraordinary." Then she suggested I print parts of it in SCOOP. Yeah, right! I can just see me splattering my life with Ezra all over the pages of SCOOP. Maybe she wants me to publish my diary too? After all, passages about Brad would be a great read! No?

I thanked her properly, but said "no way." I told her the story on bullying was soon to appear in SCOOP and it was written on behalf of Ezra and others like him. "It needn't be one or the other, Jennifer, you know. You could do both."

I said I'd think about it. Not.

MAY 14

Hi Dee,

Francine hasn't gone near Ezra's locker or his new backpack. She still plows into him at lunch or yanks his seat away as he's ready to plop down. "Your mother eats road kill," he hollers.

Beginning to think Pit Bull upsets me more than she does Ez. More to think about.

MAY 15

Dear Dee,

Dad's making big changes at Lauler's. Our lease expires soon, and we're moving to a more affordable space. We're increasing our line with travel accessories like backpacks and boots and money belts. Dad no longer rubs the scar above his brow.

We had our final dress rehearsal for *Fair Lady* and what a kick. I'm in all the chorus scenes and wear a white gown and silver top for the Ascot race. Brad will be coming with his buddies. Still wonder about the family.

MAY 16

Hey Dee,

Last night's performance of *Fair Lady* was awesome. At curtain call, I could see Mom and Dad together, both sets of grand-parents . . . and Ezra. Turns out they had asked Foxy if Ezra could sit in an aisle seat with Willy at his side. If either one caused a disturbance, they promised they'd quickly find an exit. Foxy gave her approval without a blink of an eye. So my brother, Ezra, was there at the end of the row stomping his feet in a standing O.

After the play, they went backstage and congratulated the whole cast. Dad had his arm resting on Mom's shoulder. I had a blast at the cast party. Brad was with us even though he wasn't in the play. He's now considered "my guy." Hope he thinks so too.

MAY 17
Hey Dee,

Finals are coming up, and the timing isn't exactly the greatest. The project will appear on the front pages of SCOOP next week. I'm so crazy busy, I'll probably bomb everything else.

MAY 18
Hi Dee,

HH, The Too Many, grudgingly agreed to include alleged reports of teacher inaction. What changed his mind? Maybe Mr. Alter? Maybe a few parents finally got through? We don't know. But whatever the reasons, hey, we'll take it, we'll take it! He still insists we say our intel is not fully confirmed and asks that we not use specific faculty names. Small concessions, all things considered. Now the project is finally ready to print, so to speak, if you will.

I must say I'm really proud of what this project says and does. With all due immodesty . . . it's first rate.

MAY 19
Hey,

In the article (in language more elegant than I use with you, Dee), I tell the story of Lenny, who goes to school each day in terror of teasing and vicious name calling. "It isn't true what they say about sticks and stones," he says, looking at the ground, "insults dig deeper than spears." We report on physical bullying where kids get kicked or shoved or literally arm-twisted into surrendering iPods, laptops, or other things of value. We describe painful cyber-bullying where false rumors are spread and humiliating photos circulated. We explode the myth that bullying is only a male sport. Though girls tend to bully through group rejection, some are not above hauling off and belting a former friend just like their male counterparts.

Finally, we recommend school-wide policy changes to be implemented ASAP!

Our anti-bullying recommendations begin with a clear definition of bullying behavior: repeated verbal, physical, or online abuse designed to humiliate, terrorize, or otherwise harm another student. We insist that students, teachers, parents, and administrators report every incident and set up a hotline for anonymous reporting. We urge teachers to take seriously each complaint and when necessary begin disciplinary measures that may include referral to a school counselor or a therapeutic facility, or eventual suspension. Nor do we give onlookers a free ride. We make clear that students who stand around doing nothing but wimping out are considered accessories and will be treated accordingly.

So how do you like them apples, Harris Harrington, The Too Much and Too Many, if you will, so to speak?

MAY 21
Dear Dee,

Today I am fifteen and in only one more year I'll be sixteen with an honest-to-goodness driver's license.

A gang of us celebrated at Second City in Chicago (a present from Mom and Dad) where a group of improv actors had us rolling in the aisles.

But the best part of this birthday was the gift from Brad: a beautiful gold necklace with "Jen" engraved on a medallion, almost shaped like a heart. I will never take it off. I will wear it to bed, in the bath, the shower, the swimming pool. I will wear it during finals, at meetings with The Too Many—wherever good luck is needed—like everywhere.

MAY 22
Dear Dee,

Since I did the actual writing for the project, the SCOOPers insisted I get an exclusive byline. In truth, a bunch of people contributed to the story and they deserve a ton of recognition. I made sure Brad and Megan's names were included in the "assisted by" category. I do have to admit it was awesome to be named *the* author.

Because my name and e-mail address appear above and below the article, messages from all sorts of kids, parents, teachers, and counselors came flooding in. Ms. Mitchell's message was over the top. "Remarkable, excellent. A professional piece of work." Kids who have been targeted in the past sent unforgettable messages. Their honesty, their courage, and their moving stories brought tears to my eyes. "Since I've read your article, I've been able to sleep through the night for the first time since summer. Now I can go to school knowing that people are finally listening and doing something to keep us safe."

I'll remember that one always.

Been thinking about writing another article reporting on those e-mails I received.

But OMG, I'd still have to deal with The Too Many.

The postings from these kids make me all the more determined to go to the best school of journalism, to be the most extraordinary investigative reporter I can possibly be. Make way, Indiana, here I come!

MAY 23
Dear Dee,

I know the project was a great success and I made Mom and Dad really proud. But most of all, I hope it will make school safer for Ez. Can't run interference next year. I'll be in a different school and one without a bridge to Ezra's.

MAY 24
Dear Dee,

Ez came home today saying that he heard my article in SCOOP might bring an end to bullying at Roosevelt. "Bulls are large male animals with very thick horns," he declared. "Bulls are professional basketball players on a Chicago team. I don't think I've seen any of these bulls at our school, Jen," he said with an almost grin.

"Kids like Francine who are mean to other kids act like angry bulls with sharp, charging horns," I say. "That's why we call what they do bullying."

"But they aren't what you think of when you think of bulls," he informs me.

"No, but Francine has behaved like a real bull most of this year, hasn't she, Ez?"

"But she isn't a four-legged bull," he insists. "She is a big, nosy, mean girl with scissors and very large feet covered by large boots."

Who can argue??

MAY 25
Dear Dee,

At lunch today, Megan and Zoe brought me a chocolate layer cake for dessert to celebrate a "terrific" job on the story. Megan did a chunk of work on the project and she deserves a large share of praise. She said she was blown away by how much ground I covered, and the real difference the articles will have on people's lives. For all my talk about jealousy, my BFFs may feel some pangs of envy, but they can still genuinely share in my success. They are pretty darn special and I'm pretty darn lucky to have them as BFFs.

MAY 28
Dear Dee,

Ms. Mitchell asked to see me after class. This time I forgot to be worried. Ms. Mitchell talks in "up speak," so every sentence sounds like a question. "Your term paper has been chosen for the Roosevelt writing award? It's given for the best essay written by a student in middle school? We will present the award to you on graduation night?" Was she asking or telling? When my heart began hop-scotching, I think I knew. She told me I have considerable talent with real promise for a career in any form of writing I choose. That's right, "any form of writing I choose." How about that?

I thanked her profusely. I was genuinely grateful. "I would never have written this essay about my brother without your encouragement, Ms. Mitchell. Much of the credit for this award belongs to you."

She nodded in agreement. WHAAAT?!?

MAY 29
Dear Dee,

Told Mom about the writing award. She swung me around the room and gave me her "I'm so proud of my Jenny" smile.

Dad put his hands on my shoulders and said, "Nothing could make me prouder than your receiving this award, my Jenny Jen."

"Even being class president?" I teased.

"Even being the U.S. president," he said with the biggest smile in the universe.

MAY 30
Dear Dee,

Ez is trying to fathom "humor." He's noticed that when people tell each other scripted stories, it makes them laugh. He doesn't know why they laugh, but he's come to believe it's a good thing. Sure, Ezra still prefers his own company, but he's beginning to feel alone when he sees others who are not alone.

So now he memorizes jokes just as he does commercials. He is not above telling an innocent bystander a riddle he doesn't at all understand. "When is a door not a door? When it's ajar."

"Hey, did you hear the one about the guy who was asked what he would do if he were chased by a bear? 'Well, I'd run,' the fellow says. 'You mean you would run with a bear behind?'" While the listener rolls his eyes, Ez bends over in laughter, trying to imitate the real thing.

MAY 31
Dear Dee,

Everyone's coming to graduation tomorrow night. And they'll all see me receive my award. Awesome. I'll see Mom and Dad sitting hand in hand, radiant, and together. Look, everyone, my parents are here side by side, just like yours. And both sets of beaming Grands will be thrilled to see Ezra there—who cares if he needs Willy at his side? And Brad will sit next to me like the proud partner of an Academy Award winner. I'll rise and hug him before I go to receive the award. NOT.

I'll glance at Ezra and wonder will he step aside in moving traffic, will he ever have a special friend? Will he ever make it on his own? Shush, Jenny. Can't fret about tomorrow. Too much right about today.

JUNE: VIVA LE EZRA

My dear Dee,

A day to remember.

They were all there as I had imagined. Mom and Dad wore nonstop smiles, warmly greeting longtime friends. Ez was in an aisle seat, Willy at his side. I could lip read him chanting his commercial riffs: Enablex, Windex, Terminix, Viagra, Aricept for Alzheimers and dementia, too. Don't think Gramps was charmed.

The auditorium was strewn with a rainbow of flowers, and families were blends of happy smiles. Soon caps and gowns were marching to the rhythms of the Roosevelt band. We all stood tall and proud, even the cut-ups who try to skip class. When the gowns were properly seated, HH gave a welcoming speech through his locked jaw. Then graduation began. The Too Many called out the first, middle, and last names of every eighth grader as though he were the voice of the BBC. "CALVIN, DOUGLAS, RUTHERFORD." When each came forward to receive a certificate, a shiver went down my spine.

Richard Kaplan gave the valedictory address, followed by Amy Woo, the salutatorian. Each gave an inspirational speech that "pointed us to tomorrow." At the end of his speech, Richard looked squarely at the graduating class as though he were a bearded professor and said "Stay in touch with the friends beside you today; they will be among the best you will ever know." He closed with a quote from Mark Twain, "To get the full value of joy, you must have someone to divide it with." Wonder what Ez was thinking.

Zoe Meader, my BFF and class president, announced a list of awards, each presented by the appropriate teacher. Mr. Parker, science; Ms. Courvier, French; Mr. Carpenter, art. Finally, Ms. Mitchell announced the middle school essay award presented to Jennifer Lauler. My family hooted and hollered as I walked to the stage. When Ms. Mitchell handed me the gift certificate, she added, "Jennifer's essay was written at the level of excellence of our best high school students." I felt myself blush with pride and embarrassment. When I returned to my seat, all the Laulers and Wilsons and even the Neuworths were whooping it up long after the crowd settled down.

There were more speeches, more self-puffery, and I stopped paying attention. While I am zoning out, I vaguely hear HH touting a project whose recommendations brought sweeping changes in the Evanston school district. Mom and Dad turn to wink at me. HH goes on to say, "The idea, the inspiration, the driving force and primary author of this project will receive the *Chicago Sun-Times* writers' award presented to an outstanding young journalist demonstrating extraordinary promise in the field of journalism. The winner will receive full tuition to Yale University's summer writing program to commence at the end of this month." Then with a grand flourish, he said, "It is with immense pleasure and personal pride that I present this award to JENNIFER LEE LAULER."

When I heard "Jennifer Lee Lauler" and "scholarship" and "writing" and "Yale," I wanted to shriek, do handstands, and jump out of my goose-bumped skin. Sure, I had an idea from the intro that he was going to recognize the project. But when I heard my name? Honestly? I was totally, absolutely, thoroughly, and completely blown away.

Then the "cord" began tugging a bit. But only a bit, because I know Ez now has Willy and Jonathan and I *will* go to Yale because I know we'll both be okay.

With knees shaking I walked down the aisle and tripped on the first step. Luckily I regained my balance and tried to look like I know where I was. HH reminded me. There he was strutting about, thumbs inside his vest, posing like he was the father of investigative journalism. When he handed me my certificate, I thanked him without using his name. I was sure "The Too Many" would pop out of my snarky mouth. I moved to the mic and recognized all the members of the SCOOP editorial board, giving special thanks to Bradley Neuworth for his good advice and generous support. A titter ran through the caps and gowns.

Then without warning, a powerful surge comes over me. Hands trembling, I remove the mic from its stand and say what I've long wanted to say out loud. "I would like to tell you about my brother, Ezra Allen Lauler, who was born with autism. But trust me, that alone will never define him. Just spend one day with him and you will see firsthand what courage is all about and what resiliency really means. Sure, I know there are others who face the same and even bigger challenges than he. But you see, Ezra is my brother and I . . . I . . . love him and I want to know he is safe, safe at school and on the street and wherever he may be. So to make sure that happens, I want to work to make this world a better place and a safer place for Ezra and others like him. The first step in that direction is the SCOOP project which just received this unbelievable honor. And I have to admit I am thrilled by this special recognition. But you see, Ezra deserves a ton of praise as well. So I would like to dedicate this award to him, Ezra Allen Lauler, my incredible brother."

Mom and Dad were weeping, his arm around her shoulder. Brad clasped his hands above his head like a prizefighter. That's when I almost lost it. "Thank you for letting me tell you about my brother," I said in barely a whisper.

The hall was totally quiet. Surely they could hear my heart. When no one said another word, I began leaving the stage. Then someone came running down the aisle shouting in a booming voice, "VIVA VIAGRA, Jenny Jen, VIVA VIAGRA!"

OMG Ezra Ez. Viva Le Ezra, my astonishing brother. VIVA . . . VIVA . . . VIVA Le EZRA!

NOTE TO READERS

There is no doubt that living with a sibling on the autism spectrum can be a challenge. In *Autism, The Invisible Cord,* Jenny writes of a host of feelings she and you likely wrestle with day after day. Jenny describes feelings that bewilder and contradict, feelings that surface without any warning. One moment she wishes her brother would live on the moon, the next she anguishes about the distance between them. At times she wants to throw up her hands and shout that it's time for Ezra to shape up and act his age. Then she marvels at how hard he tries. Jenny lives in a confusing cycle of love and anger, struggling to make them co-exist. You too may know this familiar balancing act of competing feelings. You may feel occasional guilt, resentment, or a sense of obligation towards your sibling. How do you take care of yourself and your feelings during difficult times? What can you do?

TALK WITH FRIENDS

Beginning a mutually shared heart-to-heart with a trusted friend will lighten your load and strengthen your friendship. Having a good chat with an understanding friend can allow you to release pent-up feelings, find a different slant on things, lift your mood, and make you feel as though the sun just came out. If the right friend is not available, search your family for a wise aunt or like-minded uncle, or another trusted adult. At times you may feel your parents already have enough on their plates without your being yet another burden. Extended family members, well aware of your parents' many responsibilities, can be thoughtful advisors, patient listeners more able to view your problems from an objective distance. Chances are their plates aren't stacked as high. You needn't worry about piling on more. Setting up regular visits during times you need it most can be of immense help.

BE YOUR OWN ADVOCATE

Like Jenny, you may feel that you and your sibling are connected by an invisible cord. That offered comfort at first, but has now become too confining and far less a reassuring tie. Keeping a close eye on your sibling may compromise both your freedom and his. Instead of thinking of your sibling's needs first, try becoming your own advocate. Before reflexively taking care of your sibling, consider taking better care of yourself. Spend more time with your favorite friends, clubs, sports, or music, then notice how well your sibling is doing on his own. Following your own interests and allowing them to flourish will replenish your energy and ready you for more.

STRETCH AND GROW

Your hobbies, interests, and dreams will help you develop your own natural talents, your own individuality, and bring you out from the long shadow your sibling casts. If you are drawn to drama, try out for a school play. If you dream of becoming a vet, volunteer at an animal shelter. If you like books, hang out in your local library. Anything you enjoy can be useful and enriching. Make sure you reserve time to make it happen. By saving time for what you enjoy, you will feel stronger, more independent, and on your way to feeling free.

CONSIDER JOURNAL-KEEPING OR WRITING

As Jenny makes clear, journals and diaries with lock and key are safe places to bare your soul. The very process of writing offers a chance to eavesdrop on yourself, sort out thoughts, and test false assumptions. Treat yourself to a spiral notebook for a running record of your day. Include your fleeting thoughts, private feelings, current wishes, and future dreams. Keep track of what makes you laugh or cry or happy as a clam. Review your journal at the end of the week and get to know yourself better through the story that unfolds. Being mindful of events and the feelings they stir up can help you feel more in control of your life and less at the mercy of moods you can't foresee.

MAINTAIN OPEN COMMUNICATION WITH YOUR PARENTS

In many families, parents may not always agree on how to discipline their child or what mode of treatment or schooling is best. This is no different when one child is on the spectrum! Often, clashes between parents increase, tensions mount, and tempers flare. You, like Jenny, may misread your parents' closed door rumbles as signals of an impending divorce. You may feel confused, uncertain, and resentful of decisions that may not include you. Instead of jumping to conclusions, talk to your parents and keep the lines of communication open. When you talk frankly and openly to your parents, you allow yourself to separate fact from fiction, and possibly clear away needless concerns. In turn, letting your parents know what's on your mind helps them better help you. Keeping an ongoing dialogue between you can stave off problems. Similarly, differences in attitudes toward the spectrum child may trigger conflicts between generations. Sadly, disputes between your parents and grandparents can interfere with or possibly rupture a relationship once enjoyed as a loving source of support. Unfortunately, when your family most needs a helping hand, grandparents and other family members may too often retreat. Again, talk to your parents and grandparents. Sometimes just talking can bring family members closer together and help them work out their differences.

"DEMAND" ATTENTION

If your sibling's needs seem to be preoccupying your parents, or if you feel overlooked, sit down with your parents and ask that "attention be paid." Arrange a special time with each parent and meet on a regular basis. Consider a scheduled outing like a Sunday night movie or bowling night. Family traditions— holiday baking, Mother's Day brunch in bed—can also be ways to keep connected and involved in each other's lives. If one-on-one time becomes infrequent, ask for "rain checks" no matter how stretched your calendars may be.

JOIN A SUPPORT ORGANIZATION

Organizations such as Sibshop, Autism Speaks, or local autism groups, to name a few, can be of immense help. Sibshop brings sibs of special needs children together to share experiences, voice concerns, offer solutions and have a special time with a new set of friends. There are Sibshop chapters throughout the country that can be located by contacting your regional autism organization. National organizations can keep you updated on new developments in autism, offer you reading material, and help your parents remain informed.

GET PROFESSIONAL HELP

If ever your feelings become too strong or disruptive; if you have trouble sleeping, eating, or concentrating in school; if you have trouble getting along with friends, and find little pleasure in your life, you may benefit from professional help. Talk to your parents or a trusted adult such as a favorite teacher, school counselor, or clergyman. If needed, they can refer you to the right professional therapist or counselor who can be of help. Your parents can arrange your first meeting which may later include a family session if that is considered most helpful.

WITHDRAWN